THE ANSWER

JEREMY LARNER

OTHER BOOKS BY JEREMY LARNER

DRIVE, HE SAID

THE ADDICT IN THE STREET
(*with Ralph Tefferteller*)

THE ANSWER

THE MACMILLAN COMPANY • NEW YORK

Library of Congress Catalog Card Number: 68-12931

FIRST PRINTING

The Macmillan Company, New York
Collier-Macmillan Canada Ltd., Toronto, Ontario

Printed in the United States of America

The characters, places, and incidents in this book are entirely fictitious, and any resemblance to any real people, places, or incidents is wholly coincidental.

The author gratefully acknowledges a grant from the National Endowment for the Arts.

for A.C., who thinks that men could live better

He thought he saw an Argument
That proved he was the Pope:
He looked again, and found it was
A Bar of Mottled Soap.
"A fact so dread," he faintly said,
"Extinguishes all hope!"

—LEWIS CARROLL

1

ON AN ICY AFTERNOON in the winter of 1964, three very long years ago, I was lucky enough to be in the arms of a girl I loved beneath clean sheets and many thick blankets. Yet in the middle of it all, just when I was least myself, letting loose, drifting up to the surface, I saw a little man in a waistcoat standing in a dark corner near the kitchenette.

While we'd kissed each other, dusk seeped in at the corners of the small-paned yankee windows. In rapture with her silken skin I wished I could taste her all in my mouth at the same time endlessly, never to decline into mere satiety. I wished also to see her, wished at least for a lamp above to make a cunning half-light through the covers. I would have lit a candle, a spotlight even, but Cathy likes to be secret, from herself as well, and I would not jostle her from her difficult path.

After a time she worked against me like a driven thing, inwardly possessed, eyes closed and chin locked into my shoulder. Made too soon an instrument, half wild with my power, half stupidly alone, I remembered if I went ahead the long low wait for her to follow, while I lay bored with the softness, the exquisite fleshliness I was just then mad to handle and handle and finally clutch.

What can a man do? Too young to know anything for sure, I tried to think of the awkwardness, the odd corners of hip and thigh, the veins and tubes and runny stuff within, but no luck, I was still coming on, much much too soon. Her frail legs flailed maddeningly, the insides of her thighs, and I needed nothing less than death to jellyjam my spinal relay.

What's the world's most fearful, prick-folding sight, I asked myself. As if I could believe in horror or pain or misery! Not then!

Yet something appeared, and what did it turn out to be? The man, the man. His jaws and little nose were dead white; his eyes were hidden in the shadow of his hat rim.

I had seen him before, but only in dreams. As a small boy I had dreamt myself again and again in the park beside my father, who stood lucid and furious in the border of the glareless arc-light, hands on hips for all the world to see. His eyes burned hawklike but could not pierce the deepest bush where the little man stood slowly leveling his revolver. I tried to force a cry, but the words clogged in my throat. I could not breathe, I had to wake, for a shot had been fired, a bullet hung whining in the air.

Growing older, I had forgotten. My little man remembered: he had come to see his betrayer, and watched me now with implacable hostility, for the punishment, the terror, the humiliation that must inexorably come down upon me.

What teenage drivel! Here I was bound up in the breath and bones of my lovely girl, and I had to sail off into inexorability!

But the little man worked all right. I shut my eyes in a cold sweat, pinned and covered as Cathy went into her openers. Could she tell anything at all, or was it precisely my clammy stillness that brought her on in a hurry? Whichever way, she was relieved, open, aware of me. I heard her say, "What is it, Alex?"—and her kisses like wet petals on my neck and shoulders.

"Hallucination . . . I think."

"Poor lover!"

Unfair! But she entented me in her black hair, and for once I let it be delicious. I was content to live in there, suffocated, mothered.

"What was it?"

"Won't tell."

"Did it bother you?"

"Yes a lot."

"Tell me what it was."

"Like this," I said, grabbing her shoulder and forcing her over beneath me. She was all set now I knew, and my blood flowed back, my gut unclenched, and I gave, at last, what I had come to give her. And there was attention between us; and we were grateful.

"What was it?" she said. "Can I see it too?"

"It was just one of those things," I sang her.

"Just one of those thingish things
An object or two
You hold with a screw. . . ."

"I mean really," she said.

"This is an Italian movie," I said. I went on singing, with covers pulled over my head:

"So goodbye dear hello dear in Zen
Which means we will meet round the bend
You'll stuff my pale hand
Wrist-deep in the sand
And I'll think it's the end."

She grabbed for my stomach.

"You didn't see anything!"

I curled up and let her wrestle with my back and

shoulders. I wanted her to go away, so it was okay with me when our noises reached the next room, where Cathy's baby woke from his late nap and sent out noises of his own. Cathy jumped up all skinny and quivery, not at all the same as my bunched handfuls, and blanketed herself in her winish horserobe.

"I was just kidding," I said.

"I knew you were."

She stuck her tongue out.

"Huckleberry," I prompted.

The baby was still crying. Flapping her rubber slippers, Cathy marched into the kitchenette and switched on the light. I watched her warm the nippled tube, knowing all the time I had not till then dared look there, not once.

I heard her singing as I lay in the hot sheets, a song of sailing on the winedark sea. Soon her diapered Huckleberry would come toddling out. It was understood that I retire to the bathroom, dragging with me my pile of clothes grown amazingly wide and heavy.

But at least I had blotted out my homunculus: I sat in a state of ancient Japanese No-thought, ass taking solace from the tub's cool scallop, as tenderly I soaped and resoaped my member. Cherry little bluey bathroom, shower shawl of sun-yellow! I trickled freezing water down the back of my throat, and gradually the world took on its edge again. Once more that faint gnawing resumed in my belly.

Eighteen-month Huckleberry came swaggering into the livingroom, quite sure he owned the joint and nothing in it could undo him. "Ah-uk!" he said by way of greeting, and cheerfully began to rip out books from the lower shelves. By this time the gloom was cut in cones of transecting yellow lamplight. Cathy had made tea. I grabbed the little boy and hoisted him for a swing. He laughed at first in unmatchable freedom, but was too soon awake and began to whimper. Insulted, I forced myself to look out the window. Cathy saw it all and laughed her motherly laugh. With Huck she was the only one, and she knew it. She consoled him with a word and a touch, and came to rub my shoulders as I stared out into the five o'clock February darkness. Suddenly our whole relationship seemed one long consolation.

"Alex?" she said. "What's the matter?"

"I don't know. Honestly I don't."

"I'm sorry," she said.

I gave her a kiss. There was nothing to be sorry for. I just couldn't keep it up—in six minutes I was down in the streets, sloshing and cursing my way along. To look at me you would have thought I knew where I was going.

2

I WOUND THROUGH a clutch of hoods on the corner, while they measured me ever so slightly from the corners of their eyes and held tight to their cigarettes. I was not unlike them, if only they knew. But how could I let them know? I walked instead down the long avenue which borders the college quadrangle, following the grimy trollies toward my dormitory. My fellow students passed me right and left, each to his own costume, thinking, talking, well-occupied. A white toy poodle came in ski pyjamas to sniff at my leg, winding round me a crimson umbilicus from a metal blonde in pony coat, slacks, white vinyl boots. She coyly smiled, and her face broke into a thousand pieces, sixty years old at least, but from the back a beacon for nymphet-rapers. Around her flowed the traffic of haunted academics and tidy professionals, foreign innocents, strange tough women and shiny thick-faced shopgirls on their way home to supper. Near the deep-lit subway they stopped to buy fresh magazines and newsprint, jostling arms and padded shoulders, twining hands as they squeezed with bowed heads to drop their coins.

Back in Kansas I had pictured my college as an Eastern garden, rich in dialectic, where my natural potentials would be nurtured to a verdant lustre. Since then I had read clusters of books and scribbled reams of notes from scholarly speeches. My mind had accustomed itself to a constant patching process, wherein pieces of a course or book or man were pasted to the bare bones of a theory, any theory. I began to write what were called good papers; at times it seemed I was actually learning. But suddenly, in the winter of my third year in New England and my twentieth of life, I had lost my touch for connections. Every idea by which men lived had abruptly cut loose from its moorings. I could see them, the ideas, spinning interchangeable like so many flakes of snow. Yet all around me others went on talking, asserting, apparently believing. I had begun to doubt the innateness of my innate talents. I could not speak as men and boys who drew out their words in webs of interlacing allusion, then went on to laugh at wit's first twist, all obvious to them.

It had to be more than the words themselves. Perhaps it was a different way of reading books and remembering. I know that seeing them on the street, these academic great ones, talking precisely one with another, forcing unnatural smiles, made me queasy, jealous, angry. They only pretend, I swore; they've pretended so long they no longer realize! A them-and-me division came clanking down like a set of iron bars. Yet still as I walked I checked each passing face, hoping for a flash I could not name.

Luckily I could keep this up in long fits only. Soon, I knew, some sight or sound would jar me loose from myself. I had in reserve a notion of pure action, which I played out a little at a time.

White thighs! I see a girl in short skirt and bleached leather coat half-bending as she peers into the art-and-foreign-language bookshop. She shivers, rubbing her slightly-fat knees together, as I draw near with dream of one cold hand between her smooth pale leg flesh.

Sensing me she turns—too late I know I know her.

She is a real and funny and boring and sometimes beautiful girl named Renée whom I picked up at a soda fountain six weeks earlier.

"Alex Randall! Hey I've got so many things to tell you!"

She takes my arm.

"If only you didn't hate me."

"I don't hate you." I smile nicely. "How're things?"

"What things?" she says suspiciously, and we're off to a fine start.

Renée was once queen of the prom at a school far out on Long Island, not stupid at first, but pretty and sexy enough never to have heard an honest word in her life. She had money, too, and didn't even know it. She was going through her first awakening.

"I have some very prime grass," she tells me now. Her mouth is making hurt movements. She had taken me to her room, she thought, for kicks; that is, on principle. But within a week she wanted assurances. She called me on the telephone. Once Cathy was there and picked up the receiver, leading to words and waste and ugliness. Renée came on so hip to herself—if only she really were! If she were hard as a rubber ball, like the one and only Blonde Star! (And yet inside the Blonde Star quivers, quivers, for anything tasty and true.)

"I know you're not interested," says Renée.

She says it very straight, turning to go, and I notice I cannot walk away. I don't want to have to hurt her—or to let her forget. Pathetically I grab her arm.

"No, I am, really, I am very interested," I lie, and probably would go right through to the grubby end of it, with her holding on and saying when will she see me, and me jumping to flee from the posters, the records, the bedspread, the toy dolls—her whole apparatus.

"I won't make it hard for you," she says. "Don't you have an appointment or something?"

She's right: I do! My face lights up in an idiotic smirk.

"I can imagine," Renée says, giving me the righteous eye, the hurt mouth, the half-turn of the shiny-coated thrust-up young breast. I put my hand on her hip. I really want just to squeeze her in my fingers.

"Well," she says, "if you don't want . . ."

"I don't," I say, "I mean I can't. Be good. Please. See you later."

—As if I really were the heartless bastard of her dreams, able to turn and leave without the slightest recognition of her "When?"

Happy me, to be telling her for once the truth: I had promised to visit my father, whom I had not seen since Christmas. I stride through the slush in surprising elation.

He had called the night before, to summon me by super-phone, his new plaything on which he could ring anyone anywhere and blast off as long as he liked for one flat tax-deductible fee. He would be visiting the big city across the river, he informed me, and would expect me for dinner at five o'clock in his suite at the Commander Arms.

The old hotel gave off a brown-yellow light from its bay windows, standing at attention in a little square, bundled up to its balconies in Colonial brick, top-heavy, epauletted, buttressed below with rich worn lobbies. In the carriage-style elevator I got out my wallet and peered in the dimness of madeover gaslamps at a snapshot of my father as I preferred to remember him.

The photo was taken in a mechanical booth in the Ft. Smith bus station in 1936, when my father was about the age of a college freshman. My Dad was a religious young Okie in possession of illustrious ambitions. Though born and bred a brush-town Baptist, he wanted to become an Episcopalian priest. He reckoned he was ready for something a little grander, he'd told me the only time we ever spoke of it, on the day twenty years later when he was cleaning out his deal bureau and I fished up the snapshot from the wastebasket. For him the photo was all used up; for me it was a relic.

Just to "get things straight," he told me how, on a winter's day in the middle of the Depression, young Arthur Randall hitched into Fort Smith in his one funeral suit and turned his cardboard collar around in the photo booth to provide the first and last evidence of his self-ordination. Two hours later he embarked on his pilgrimage to the Episcopal seminary in Pudendo Beach, California.

No difference that the subtle seminarians laughed at him and turned him away for lack of an entrance fee. No difference my own secret laughter later. For the photograph itself was a remarkable artifact, a triumph of gauche nerve over reality. The face was that of a consummate young Jesuit, spiritually undefiled, whose shrewd fierce gaze bespoke a soul full of destiny. And the jaw was there, even then, but cleaner, younger, more kissable.

The jaw said that Arthur Randall would bull his way through. Not that he didn't kick around for a while: as scenery-cleaner, shad-boner, grunion-dealer, and in his spare time as a member of a brief but widespread California moon cult. Later on he worked his way back East through one failed business after another, arriving in Oklahoma in time to slip a year and a half of college between himself and his draftboard.

But the Depression couldn't beat him, couldn't dent that jaw, nor the War, nor his own false starts afterwards.

Eventually he had built, "with my own hands," a simple factory, and parlayed it, in three quick years, into a string of warehouses through which he cornered the market on ingredients and sold them at twenty-five times cost. Personally I couldn't care less about ingredients. But when he wasn't around, I thought well of the old man.

When I knocked my father called "Come in," and I found him stretched out on the pre-Raphaelite plush couch, his crossed legs over the armrest, his Stetson perched on one of the doilies, dressed in a pair of mesh underpants ordered by the gross from Abercrombie-Fitch: my sunbronzed wedge of a dad, muscles barely beginning to crinkle on the backs of his arms and down the middle of his chest.

And such somnolent sad blue eyes, with lashes drooping like an old-time vamp! He was terribly hurt, he let me see that right away, even as I smiled in admiration.

He got up slowly, nodding his head to himself, gave me a bear hug, rubbed his knuckles on my head, and retreated with fists on hips.

"I guess it was something pretty damn important," he said, still nodding. His eyes fixed me in a baleful glare.

"Sorry I'm late," I mumbled. Carefully avoiding the couch I flopped into one of the old-maid armchairs, with a doily for my precious neck and high-walled sideboards to protect me.

My father snorted. He sat down on the coffee-table, still staring sadly, like an outgrown underpant ad.

"It's only six," I said; "only five in Kansas City. We can still have a good supper together."

"I ate," my father said. He waved towards the corner, where a bellhop's cart sat draped with a grey sheet. "I couldn't be sure you were coming. And I don't think I understand that crack about Kansas City."

He had been leaning back with his arms stretched behind him and his chest stuck out, but now he put his elbows on his knees and pointed his jaw at me.

"Are you waiting for me to explain it?"

He smacked his first into his palm. Despite myself, I jumped. My father was on his feet and grimly nodding his head.

"Well," he said. "I guess I know where I stand!"

I thought that made a pretty fair beginning.

"It's nice to see you, Dad, you're looking good."

"Lost four pounds down in Nay-saw. Up every morning and run two miles on the beach."

He walked thoughtfully on the carpet, rubbed his chest, worked his jaw silently and lay down on the couch again.

"Were you with that little Irish girl?"

I didn't answer. I was contemplating a brisk run down the fire escape.

"Tell me candidly son, what do you see in her?

"I know of course you're not going to answer that," he said. "I understand you on that, son. I think you and I think pretty much alike, basically.

"She does have an uh . . . illegitimate . . . doesn't she?"

"I told you before she was married and divorced."

"And you knew her husband?"

"Very well."

"What was he like?"

"Confused. Too young. A grad student who wasn't making it. He got upset and ran away."

"Huh!" he snorted. "What's that?"

"I told you before, I'm pretty sure. He ran away about a year ago."

"Did he indeed? Indeed!"

His mesh-sheathed scrotum rested lightly on the

tabletop. I could've brought my fist down and cracked his balls like a bag of nuts.

"Indeed," I said.

"And that doesn't make you think! Not one little bit!"

"As a matter of fact, it does."

"Huh! What about?"

"What they were like."

"What? It doesn't make you think about this young girl, about the kind of man she gets involved with?"

"What kind of man is that?"

"Kind of man who might be just a little weak, a little young, not ready for . . . commitment."

"—And she devours them, like a vacuum-cleaner. Irish girls do that."

"I didn't say that, son. No need to get touchy. I understand exactly how you feel. Don't forget I went to college myself. Plenty of these little broads would have given their right arm! But no siree! I knew what I wanted. You had to, in those days, or the Depression would deal you right out of the deck. I had to have a woman who would appreciate my goals. The first split-second I spotted my little gal, I said to myself, there goes the mother of my sons!"

"So you understand," I said.

"I do, son, believe me." He laid his hand on my shoulder, whapped me in the small of the back, and moved on.

"Only one thing that gives me trouble, son, when all's said and done."

He waited.

"Alex, don't you want to work?"

"I'm getting hungry," I said.

"Huh! Look son, there's a certain amount of work to do in this world—"

"And every man that really is a man wants to do his share of it," said I, rising.

He came up close and I backed away to lean uncomfortably against the low dresser.

"I don't know, son. All I know is this: no one sent me money from home, not one thin dime! My parents were decent people, but they had all they could do to put food in their own mouths and my brothers' and sisters'. And damn lucky at that, in those days, with a lousy little hardward store and no guts or imagination!

"That football scholarship meant something to me. It was my meal ticket. Many a times when I was sick or feeling not so hot, you can bet I damn well went ahead with it. And was a better man for it! I had pride," he said, *"in here,"* tapping his heart. "I wasn't about to get spoiled," he said. "It was march on or fall by the wayside.

"Now the old man will admit he was kind of proud when you got your scholarship. Especially to a school like this, regardless what kind of teams they have. But what he never will understand is—"

"Why I gave it up."

"What?"

"I gave it up because I was mediocre."

"You were all-Kansas!"

"But *really,* I was mediocre."

"You were as good as any back in the East."

"And I had other things to do."

"Like fool around?"

"I don't know. Like books to read."

"Hum!"

He couldn't come out against books. He began to walk around the room, while I slipped to the floor and sat with my legs drawn in. He began to talk about my sister, who was about to graduate high school. It seemed she had been going out with a college boy who was "intelligent, all right, no doubt about that. But Alex, you should see that scruffy whelp. He walks and talks like a scruffy whelp. Whines his words from the corner of his mouth, won't look you in the eye, keeps one hand in his nose and the other in his ear. But Donna thinks he's 'sincere'! He's sincere all right! You should see his family. His father's a brilliant professor but he can't even stand up and shake hands like a man. The first wife divorced him—not that I blame her—but she left the kids with *him*—and if you meet them, you could appreciate that too. What a *sick* family! Their house smells so bad you can hardly breathe the air. I guess it's from all that sincerity!

"Well I suppose your sister's going through a stage. I can understand that. It's a stage, wouldn't you say so?"

He was relenting, playing for my sympathy. The hurt had been switched to my sister.

"I know I'm unreasonable," he said. "I guess every father is. You raise a kid and you want her to have what she's got coming. But no . . . it's more than that . . ."

He sank down on the couch and closed his eyes. Physically he was still young and strong, but there were lines around his eyes that ran straight across the lids. It occurred to me he was the kind of man who has a coronary before he's fifty.

"You're tired, Dad."

"I guess I am." He smiled wanly, showing me his small sharp teeth. "I appreciate your concern, son. The truth is I have trouble controlling myself. I'm not so dumb I don't know that. I have trouble separating the big things from the little things, and I tend to forget that everything's going to work out all right in the end. And damn it, I shouldn't ought to let myself!"

He let out a terrific sigh.

"You believe that, don't you son?"

"What?"

"That everything happens for the best, or can be made to?"

"There's always another possibility."

"And what's that?"

He leaned forward, a friendly frown pin-striping his tanned brow.

"Oh, I don't know," I said. I sighed myself.

"I don't know either, son." My father smiled warmly.

He reached out to take my hand, but I was too far away. He took his own hand.

"It's hard to maintain perspective," he said. "I do all right in business but I know I pay for that by losing out with you kids. And having Big Billy off in Viet Nam doesn't help things either. I suppose that's what really sets me off inside, having him out there and never knowing."

For the first time I wanted to say something, but there was nothing to say.

"You don't write to him, do you? You haven't had a letter? I can't reach him—I even tried by phone—and he never writes, not a word!"

My father laughed. "I never write myself—must run in the family. But you know how my little gal worries!"

"Hey!" he said, "you want a drink?"

He went to the bellhop's push-table and uncovered an opened bottle of bourbon. He poured two inches' worth over melted ice-cubes.

"You know what that scum wants her to do?"

He leaned at me over the cart. I thought at first he meant my brother Billy.

"Donna's friend? The sincere one?"

"By the way, don't ever mention I told you this. I'm

not even supposed to know. Your mother told me. But your sister would feel crushed if she knew I knew."

"Yes?"

"What?"

"What does he want her to do?"

"Why he wants her . . . to get in bed with him, that's what! Can you imagine it? That scum! He never even played a game in his life!"

"And what does Donna want?"

"She doesn't know. So far she's thinking it over. But he's working on her all the time. *He* knows I know it. I let him know just by the way I look him in the eye!"

"Doesn't sound so unusual though . . . when you come to think of it."

"Huh! Unusual? Not at all! Not if he were normal! If he were normal he wouldn't come sneaking about it, not with a girl he *knows* has not been so far that type of girl. Now that I'd swear to. Now you and Billy never had any secrets, up till Billy went away and I found out some things afterwards, some little wenches came to me, but it was always that other type, even then. Even then."

He fell to musing.

"Not that I blame this scum in a way. If only he weren't *sincere*. Because Alex, you should see her. Things have changed since you've been away. Your sister is really . . . well, she's stacked, if I do say so myself!"

"Kind of makes you wish . . ." I didn't quite know how to put it.

"Yeah!" he said. We had another drink. We were pals again. Suddenly he put his hand on my shoulder, and his eyes were searching mine. He needed something, so badly. Something I was going to deprive him of, it seemed. What in the devil did he need!

"You know," said my father slowly, "you feel you're

with a boy his whole life, know everything he's going through, how he feels, what's going on in his head. Then all at once he shuts you out—and he's got to!"

He backed off with his chin held in a kind of triumph.

"I understand that, son. Don't forget I've dealt with a lot of people coming down the pike."

He jabbed me on the upper arm. I winced and he moved backwards, nodding his head.

"But I just wish I knew what I did wrong!

"Because somewhere I went off the track with you two boys. . . ."

He let out air again and shook his head from side to side. Almost I spoke out in anger, but he grinned as openly as a kid.

"Let's Indian-wrestle!" he said.

So I braced my shoe against his bare foot, and rolled back my sleeve to press my hairy forearm against his tanned and shaven one. The muscles he clenched were firm, but the skin was a little loose and I did not like the feel of it. I pulled back and he easily shoved me off balance.

Then I went to it harder and we grunted in a bony vise, vibrating to subtle shifts which we instantly countered and checked in our mutual grip. I couldn't see right. Our locked hands were giving off a blinding glare. I saw only bits and pieces; my eyes focused in jumps. Slightly below there were dots of sweat along the line where my father's flecked brushcut sprouted from his forehead; I followed one drop as it rolled down a seam in his cheek and into his chincleft. He had bunched muscles twitching along his collarbone where my own flesh slackened in vulnerability. I had to apply my size and leverage before it was too late: I reached back for an extra thrust, bearing down with all my might. But he held like an oak, my old man. He countershoved; I teetered, brushed his thigh, but managed to recover. We held at stalemate. It was like pushing against a steel wall. He can't keep it up, I thought, glancing down at his purple swollen neck-veins; but just then he gave a shrug and a shove from a new direction. I flipped backwards as if shot from a catapult.

As I lay on the floor in patches of sweat my cheery, red-faced father extended a paw to help me up. For a second I was nearly happy.

But the old man said, "That was a thrill, son. You really challenged me physically. Pretty damn strong, you know, I might not win the next time. But of course you haven't been through the physical development I have, even at forty-five.

"Hey, how's your weight these days? Look a little puffy there." He pinched around my ribs, hurting me. Really hurting me.

"Now my boy Ted, my number one Junior Exec, you should see him Alex! Hard as a rock. Played top semi-pro up in Calgary."

He flopped back on the couch, winded at last.

"Only thing that shakes you up, man of my age, is when your friends start in to die on you. You can work with the weights every day of your life, and it helps your chances, God knows, but it's not an ironclad guarantee. Remember Will Myerson, Myerson and Sons? The boys run the business now, built houses for themselves too. Pretty good boys. But that old man Myerson was a wonder. They say he ran away from the Cossacks to come to this country. He had the locker next to me at the club, and Alex, he made me look like a shrimp next to him. I never saw a physique like that old man had. I bet you don't even know he's dead? No?"

I hadn't known. The lukewarm bourbon fumed in

my empty stomach. Why did I always eat or drink the wrong thing? I didn't want to hear this story.

"—you get a body like that only by forty years of weights and swimming, five–six days a week. Wasn't muscle-bound, either—could turn a front or backflip standing in his streetclothes without missing a puff on his cigar. And Alex, get this: he was a neat, clean man, meticulous about his personal appearance. Why he didn't look a day older than I do. But it got to him all the same."

My father lapsed into a kind of reverie.

"How?" I demanded.

"Choked to death on a piece of steak."

A great bit! I gave a loud cackle.

"Huh! You think it's funny. It wasn't funny in the slightest. I got there just after it happened. There was a crowd of people milling around like sheep, and in the middle his wife stood bawling. The new one, she had on a green silk dress, had herself all dolled up for a big night. They brought out Myerson on a stretcher. All covered up. And some kids began laughing, older people too, like a bunch of goddam ninnies!"

He shook his head doggedly. "Just like you, I guess. Didn't know any better. But I was thinking, you know? A man can't help thinking. *What a goddam way to die,* I kept thinking. Work all your life and this is what you come to!"

"Just as good as any," I said.

"HUH!"

He stared at me coldly, then looked down, possibly from grace, but I'm really not sure he heard me. He sat staring at his slablike hands as they squeezed and kneaded one another.

I waited squirming.

"Alex, do you believe in God?"

"No. Do you?"

"Course not. Never pretended to. Not since *you* were old enough to know the difference. Ever remember me pretending?"

"No."

He glanced at his wristwatch of spun gold, got slowly to his feet, and began to button on a nylon shirt he'd had drying on a doorknob.

"Got some people coming in a few minutes, couple of district managers I invited down. Funny, most of 'em are older than me. But you can't beat that experience, it adds a dimension. . . .

"Why am I saying this?" He stared at me blankly.

"Oh. Point I wanted to make, was to explain why the old man was a little grouchy when you let me down on the suppertime. Then too a man doesn't like second place—especially when he's your own Dad."

He buckled his belt and looked even trimmer. The top of his pants never slid out from under, as mine did.

"By the way, you know you can always turn to me, son. . . ."

I sucked at my miniscule icecube, thinking that both of us were played out, before long I'd be back on the sidewalk.

"Are there any problems?" he was saying.

"Not especially."

"Well let me know if you ever feel stuck in a situation. With women especially. There's more ways out than a younger man might think of. Now I want to make it clear I'm not advising you to take advantage. But I know sometimes a guy, if he's a decent guy, can feel obliged when he's really not."

Snow was falling again outside the window. It had been snowing all through the sleepless edgy month of mid-year exams. The day before it had rained, and snowed, and rained again. The streets of our little town were a dismal mess of frozen slush and muck and dog-turds.

"Someday son we've got to have a real good talk."

I couldn't recall the exams I had taken. For question after question I had fitted fragments of pre-stored answers. Eventually the questions stop and they let you outside again. Through the snowscreen of my tired mind I saw drifting townie faces, grey, puffed, with networks of red string arteries.

"You're not giving an inch, are you son?"

I must have flinched. He let go of his anger and went on talking.

"Well I know how it is, more or less. A man has certain needs. There's a kind of loneliness a man can't control. I know with me—" He glanced at me quickly, looked away. He would offer something: *he* could give an inch.

"You know, sometimes you travel on the road, selling, buying, talking just for the sake of talk, and no matter how much money you have, there's that ache inside you. You'd be surprised what some of these guys do. They turn into farmyard animals, lose all their self-respect. For instance—" He shifted his weight, curled up with palms together under his head—"they're after me, pretty often, to go into bars, you know, to pick up women. God knows there's plenty available, especially at my price level. I always say no. They kid me about it, but I think a man loses something priceless with things like that. He loses his dignity."

A wave of excitement passed over me. I was paying attention. "Um hmn," I said.

"In other circumstances, though, it can be enjoyable. . . ." He jerked his chin down, flashed his bright eyes right into mine.

"And what's more, I've done it!"

Well! That was a great relief. But I showed him nothing.

He leaned forward at me, mouth and forehead puckered up severely.

"Now if you ever mention a word of this to my Mary, who is a great gal by the way, and you know damn well how I love my little gal—"

I didn't give one shit how he loved his little Mary. Lucky for me his employees burst in at that moment, with hearty cries of, "Art! Big Daddio! How's the bossman tonight!"

There were three of them, clad in gabardine and mohair and silk worsted, walking flatfooted and thumping my father's arms.

He was beaming and nodding his head.

"Boys, I want you to meet my little son. The big one's all tied up tonight in Asia."

One by one they advanced and pumped my hand, lowering their barbered heads to give me a good sober onceover. My father meanwhile produced some bottles I had not seen before.

"Hey Alex!" he cried. "This character here works for Bunny's Dad. He counts the money, and every tenth bill he puts in his pocket."

"That's right, son," the character said. "And every twentieth bill I pass to your Dad."

"You ever see Bunny?" my father asked.

"I'm on my way to see him now."

"I'll just walk you out," my father said quickly. "Mix your own, boys!"

"Nice meeting you Alex!"—"Same here young fella!" etc etc.

Out in the hall my father rubbed his hand tenderly down my sweater sleeve. He had that terrific hurt look again, which caused me to throw on my coat and stamp my feet, glancing down the corridor as he barred my way.

"You know son, you knew you might be meeting friends of mine. You might've at least got a haircut, and I know damn well your mother fits you out with plenty of ties."

"Thought you might like me as I am," I shot back—and bit my lip.

For the first time he thrust his jaw in real fury. "So that's how it is huh? A one-way street!"

Involuntarily I stepped back.

"No Dad, not exactly. But as long as we're at it, I wish you'd lay off for awhile. I won't forget you, you can ease your mind about that. But that phone of yours is giving me the willies. I expect it everywhere I go. Every phone is a bomb. I cover it with a sheet before I go to bed at night."

Dad didn't smile. "So that's how it's to be!"

"No, no, no!—not how it's to be! Stop that toying, won't you please please stop it!"

But his jaw was thrusting furiously, and in a flash I was truly angry.

"All right. Yes," I said. "I'll just do without a father."

He took a step toward me, mouth open, and I put my hand on his chest and shoved him back.

My father stood clutching his breastbone and glaring with excruciating hurt—as Bunny's father's bookkeeper opened the door with a drink in his hand.

"Come on 'n join the party, Arthur!"

I walked rapidly down that grooved hall carpet, saw a little red light and dove on through fire doors and down the stairs. I had hurt him again: after all my care I had gone and hurt him again. I hated that hurt with a fury. Whenever it came out I could feel the same thing stirring in myself, like a swallowed mirror. The need, the need!

Even in the soppy, glaring street I heard the echo of that flatulent sobriety: “A man has certain needs.”

I wanted to obliterate myself, my past, my father, and most of all that need.

3

CHEZ BUNNY: an elaborate twisting of hand-made cigarettes. “Ah, the good gold,” says one green Ivy. My friend Seymour, having supplied the material for his modest fee, turns on me a physiognomy of significance, to mark with faintest lip of scorn the verbal uncool.

Bunny fits each slim stick precisely, depositing a neatly-growing pyramid, just as his counterpart of forty years ago arranged cookies on a plate for his tutors.

At length Bunny passes the top joint to Seymour, who takes it brushing back a soft lock of hair, licks the stick to a sensuous firmness, and sets it between the surfaces of his lips. Bunny lights it for him from his instrument of dull gold. There follows the ceremony of the first drag. Delicately expanded, Seymour turns his spherical back upon Bunny and breath-tight, in-sniffing, gives me a sure pass, left palm up thumb and two fingers to my right hand palm down pinch.

I respond despite myself to Seymour's perfect touch, his sense of decent ritual. And his singling me as first in line. After me the others, from the floor or on couches, leaning on elbows, eyes-closed and sucking each in turn, nodding assent to the music, reach for the next joint as it comes. Last of all our host, the strong-browed Bunny, solemn as Sir Lancelot, sucks sincerely, his lashes drooping upon large, clear eyes, as he sights true down his straight strong nose at the fine armor of nobility: his turtleneck dickey, his soft cord double-breasted, his wide belt snug on slim hips, his guerdening buckle, gentle bell-bottoms, sweater-matched socks, easy desert boots. Complete young thoughtful sensitive: the smooth brow puckers as his pink pure mouth draws intoxication to the vacuum within. Likewise my own.

A clopping without! I throw open the bulky pane and lean out on the gable, let filthy snow come benedicting head and shoulders. New snow feathers on the pocked ice shingles; up from streetwell comes honking of traffic slide over in the square. Below, prancing dappled through streetlights, a horse appears, mounted by blobular man with cap in the middle, humping his saddlehorn in hopes of catching a brace of swaybacked fluffrumps cantering on ahead. Behind me, the smell of burning hay. I belly-flop on the windowsill, in mellow jumpiness of elevation, eager to look down.

I see a robe emerge from shadows, a beaver hat and flossy black beard: the local Rabbi, harmless, his flat prints vanishing behind him as he marches on his way to God. On his way or in his groove? Seymour would say in his groove, he digs people swinging in their separate grooves, each truth to its own tunnel. That wouldn't do for the Rabbi, not if I were he.

And where was my drunk man, who'd sat propped against the wall outside the cafeteria, upturned hat in lap and barmy smile? A deplorable specimen, he caused the turning-away of stern youth faces as they came and went. But amazing to me he had scorned the private drunk, stowed safely in the secrecy of suicide rented room! Most bravely he faced them in his remarkable overcoat, with more piss than you'd think possible trickling twenty feet down stony stairs. He staggered me: to think he could still define a scene and hope to make it. He was actually getting something from the outside world—something he alone had learned how to want.

I might have seen him now with a little sunshine. He must have been in the dark, my drunk, behind the double doors which blasted light as boys swung in and out. In the pale blue lamplight I saw snowflakes glitter in their hair as they wound on scarves, jammed gloves, and strolled hunched in sportsjackets. No overcoats for them. Some with girls: bright tired ones not unlike Cathy in tan coats, or else a few with baby knees bare and high boots catching the plump of the calf just so. Lungs snugly roaring, I could have flown through the speckled air to pull down a package of slick tight empty. The sound track called for outrage of shieking righteous rape, but I guessed instead a whimper filter though my gut and beneath me the sorry softness of a melting. While from the record player: "I want to love a little girl like you/ Oh yes I do oh yes I do do do." Thumpy-bump/ thumpy-bump—and it's Love!

Popping, drifting, a motorcycle slid round the corner and spluttered up to the curb in front of Hyman's Heroes. I leaned out to my loins, looking to see if the rider were my roommate Benjy Adoremus, unseen by me for three–four days. All semester my old-line American Portuguese friend had divided his life between bike and bathtub. He had taken the mid-year's on nothing but amphetamine and the remnants of a brilliant prep-school education. Then trickled away, perhaps to Mommy in the Bahamas, perhaps to Paris or Tangier, perhaps straight down the drain and through the pipes to the roiling winter river.

But that needn't be, I vowed; not for Benjy, certainly not for my high-flying self. Or was that another man, a littler man, behind the swinging door, ready to gun me down from the black? More air! I recognized a piece of paranoia. What was it then at Cathy's, pot-free and ready for love? I had to find that out, and I could, I would. As soon as I could shake free and think. I had not yet thrown off the episode with Arthur. So much to shake, so much to throw, so little I cared to hold onto. Except one conception I seemed (miraculously) to have had all along, popping up now like a fulfillment in my moment of exaltation. Why not bring it out, the real thing, deep-seeded in me from the beginning, having nothing to do with fathers or nightmares or obligations, now if ever, before I blew the whole bit? I put my teeth together like a tough guy. After all, I was a tough guy. I could make my way. I will stop at nothing, I practiced. There has got to be something more. Big Plans would soon come to me: write an Epic, live an Epic. Become the self I believed in.

In the room, we cool ones wavered to and fro, ranging spokelike from the axis of the stereo. I saw us flung out on the couch, the beds, the flowered carpet; our shirtsleeves loose, vests unbuttoned, ties stuck in pen-pockets, legs bent and folded in a terrific casualness. I could see us in a photograph—a family portrait for the morning paper in Kansas City, where Bunny's father ran a men's accessory business. "Ivy League Drug Ring," Bunny's Mommy would read in horror, our school's good dean in embarrassment, the trustees in mortal indignation. But back in Kansas City I could hear the snickers of certain fourteen-year-olds, as they scrutinized the wirephoto for flaws in our technique. They had doubtless served up the Answer Drug at their Sweet Thirteen parties.

Seymour was taking—Seymour the Serene, as Benjy called him—a honeyed, throaty mass of mouthings slid upon my ears. Seymour lolling, talking good trips, bad trips, visions, scenes, enclosed by acolytes who listened in an agony of restrained approval.

Seymour reclined on a tapestried couch, his bulk looming resplendent in lilac shirt, fawn suede vest and checkered gaiters. Seymour's heavy head lay on a purple plush cushion, his blond straight hair falling in a gentle stream from the outskirts of a small bald spot, weaving a flaxen gauze about his thick neck, softening the thrust of his bullet dome. My feelings for my fair friend were usually mixed, but at heights like this I was impressed by the sheer luxury of being Seymour. I dug then so wistfully his natural ability to let go all pre-set distaste—and to take it all in, whatever, each for the taste of it, and that was enough. If you were truly able.

"Dr. Jim was leaving for the convention in San Fran-cisco," Seymour drawled. "I was like standing by in the loft while he dismantled his apparatus and packed up his briefcase. Something else! One by one he would stash these vials and tubes and bottles, with weird capsules stuffed full of colored grains and like powders all weighed out on his silver microscale. He would show me each pill and say like you know this, and you know this, and I would say yes, baby, um-hmn."

Seymour laughed, coughed, laughed; the porcelain faceflesh bunched rimless octagons, pushing vibrations through the fleshdeep bands and out behind his pink shell ears. Yet not a drop of perspiration soiled the red and white hairless smoothness of his cheeks.

"Finally he picked up a spansule the size of a goiter, full of little green and violet marbles. He says, you *can't* know this one, and I had to confess, man, I don't. He says, it's MNX, and I say oh! MNX! Then I say, like MNX? I mean, what is it?

"He says, Maaan" (and Seymour drew it out, leering, his sharp pigs' eyes like points of pink pencil), "if you take this, you'll be a . . . hu-man veg-table . . . for the rest of your days."

We caught giggles in the tops of our throats, giggled and giggled to think of a hu-man veg-table.

"And I say I don't get your point, Jim, I mean why would anyone want to take a dose like that?"

"He says, I don't ask questions, man; I just supply the trade!"

We wheezed, rolled, bent in formal laughter. We shook our heads. "Too much, man!"

"MNX may be the added ingredient," I said.

"What added ingredient?" asked an Indian from India.

"What added ingredient!" Seymour said.

"The ingredient," I said.

"You dig?" said Seymour.

Half of them nodded.

"What added ingredient?" said the Indian.

"You've heard of the Answer Drug?" I said.

The Indian sneered. Of course he'd heard of the Answer Drug. The Indian elite knew all about that typical American hangup. In 1964, of course, it had not too long ago begun. The scene was talked-about, but not too typical. Bear that in mind in all that follows.

"What *kind* of Answer Drug, man?" said Seymour.

"The new kind," I said, "has an added ingredient."

"Which kills body odor," said Seymour.

"And stops bad breath right in your mouth."

They froze for an instant. Bunny's eyes wandered toward his coffeetable magazine. In a second he might flip right through and find out what was or was not truly new, plus the package it came in and how to use it for getting laid.

Seymour serenely picked up the magazine and handed it to Bunny. "Page 239," he said, "in the rundown on Alienation."

Bunny bunny-laughed. His phonograph told him it was his party, he could cry if he wanted to.

It was cruel, it was shallow, it didn't come off. The walls were oppressing me. Bunny had got on another record, full of songs by the lads we all adore. Because they know the score. They've got it beat, it falls at their feet, but do they care? Gracefully they twinkle up their noses, pitter-pat for some tasteful romping. Swing the swings, slide down the slides. Put down the reporters and their come-on questions. They only love you all the more. They've never seen your like before. And all the time you're sending us your signals.

You can communicate, it is said, without words, without symbols, without trying, without meaning. Then tell us, is it coming soon, in my time, that one great scene where all the somebodies turn into the only everybodies partaking each and every one of the bloodless body the wordless word the true cool true?

At least I could be free, I thought, if the others were. Could operate with my own true self, when chains were lifted and games brought to an end. My own making it was not disconnected from the making it of others.

Basically I was very depressed, as we say, when Seymour nodded his head toward the phonograph.

"Another dimension," he said to me alone.

"Just in the music," I said.

Seymour shook his head one-half of an inch.

"Something else."

"You sure of that?"

"Surest thing I know," he brought out, in his low slurred speech.

What was the surest thing I knew?

I got to my feet and raised my hands in blessing.

"Youth of the present," I said, "I stand before you, man and boy, a living testimony to the power of baking soda. As I look about this splendid auditorium, I see your smiling upturned faces, yes, like petals on a bough, and I realize that the future lies before us, and you are the wave of that future."

Noises, ignore them. A few neat thrusts of the knee. Seymour's knowing glazed attention.

"And I must admit it, lads and laddies: my own generation, we of the horseless carriage and aspirin with added painkillers, we, well, we've made a pretty fair mess of it. My head is bowed, my feet are shuffled. But dammit, we didn't have the advantages we've given you young hermaphrodites, and what's more, fought for 'em, too, and where called upon by God and country, hacked our way through a wall of living flesh!

"Now I do not come before you with an easy solution. I would not be so naive before a group of your stature. But this I do affirm. Only this. That I like cottage cheese.

"Or maybe I don't like cottage cheese. Maybe I like cleaning fluid with platformate, or vaseline, or chlorine gas, or glue. Maybe I like nembutal with 7-Up in a no-cal rectal douche.

"But cottage cheese, my friends, is Freedom! And Freedom, my friends, is not for the weak, for the shirkers, shrinkers and malingerers who let George do it and hold out their apronstrings to the bottomless porkbarrel. No, my friends! Freedom floats ever in the curds of Responsibility!

"And I like Robittusin, my friends, I like butane balls, my friends, and I . . . like cottage cheese!"

Someone turned the phonograph up and down, blast and out, hitting the electric clubfoot.

Seymour rose in waves, chanting: "Holy Holy Holy Holy Holy Holy Holy Holy Holy Holy Holy Holy Holy Holy Holy Holy Cottage Cheese! Hare Krishna Hare Krishna Krishna Krishna Hare Hare Hare Rama Hare Rama Rama Rama Hare Hare Cottage Cheese! Plena Gratia

Ave Virgo Sanctus Sanctus Benedictus Fructus Ventris Cottage Cheese!"

At this I had to interrupt him. "Young youth," I said, and I sang him a song:

> Only Pod is Holy
> Merciful and Mighty
> Pod in Three Parsnips
> Blossoms trailing free!

As I asked that all assembled rise and join their voices in our choral anthem, a messenger burst in at the door. Bunny plunged for the toilet, where he flushed down a week's allowance. All for nought: the Enforcers were far away and otherwise occupied. The newsflash was that Benjy had taken a stupendous dosage of the Answer Drug, and was tearing around campus "panicked out of his skull." Our tale-bearer flopped down in happy panting; there was silence for a moment and then my little friends began to giggle. Soon they were in raptures of hysteria.

4

I FOUND BENJY far out on a footbridge over the river. He had climbed the stone wall of the bridge and stood catatonic as snowflakes settled into his eyelashes and dusted lightly his thin shoulders. He gazed entranced while bands of moonlight bounced from the river and radiated up his chest along his neck and out to the point of his upturned chin. Though dressed only in shirt, tie and PJ pants, he stood untrembling with his bare feet flat on the stone cold wall.

Creeping closer, I saw the feet arch up till only his toes made contact. Benjy had his arms out to the moon, swooning over the river as if to clutch it from the sky.

I grabbed him by the shirt-tail and we crashed together to the sloppy bridgewalk. For ten minutes I had a terrific fight to keep him down. Every time I'd throw him back he'd pop up and break free of me. The little guy was full of joy, like zero-eyed Annie yelpin' Leapin' Lizards at the smoke of true blue killers' machineguns. While I got soaked cold he carried on fresh as ever, hot as a fire, his little heart tripping like a telegraph key. The bridge lights streamed out curtains of snow, cutting us off from either shore, marooning us in a box of stone and sky and river. Thickening snow pressed down on us, soaking up the thuds and grunts of battle and blotting the loon song of Benjy as fast as he sent it up.

On his fifth try he practically made it over the parapet, so as I pried him loose from a lamppost I came on like Bogart Cagney, slapping him twice for his own good in the good cause.

Benjy didn't follow the script, which called for a startled stare then dawning realization. Without transition he shrank back sobbing. "I'm sorry!" he cried, in a voice so pitiful it made me want to crawl under the snow. "I didn't mean it. I won't . . . I can't. . . ."

He sputtered for breath, sobbing wretchedly. He began to writhe and thrash in the slush, despite all my efforts at soothing.

"Oh . . . oh . . . I'm sorry. . . . It wasn't me! If only you'd believe me!"

"I believe you," I said. He was beating his face into the pavement.

I pulled him upright and hugged him till the sobbing subsided. I could feel him burning through his thin wet shirt.

At last Benjy looked at me. His pupils were so wide they squeezed the irises to rims of nearly nothing. He said my name. "Hello," I said. He pinched my cheek to see if I were real.

"Let's get out of here, old friend," he said in his usual voice.

I got my coat and scarf around him, and tried in vain to tie my big shoes on his feet. He held tight to my arm. "Do you notice the snowflakes? Curious."

We plodded on.

"What's curious?"

"Way they turn. They know what they're up to. Each one is different—like us. They have six perfect sides."

"Do we have six sides?"

Benjy thought it over. "You'd be surprised," he said.

"I want to tell you a little something, Alex. I'm speaking calmly now, aren't I? As compared to before?"

"Calm isn't quite the word."

It's peculiar, isn't it? It's come down to an existential decision. Either I'm the king of beauty or the king of muck. I'm not afraid to say that now—I said it even to the Devil. But the words themselves mean nothing."

"It's all right, though. You're neither one."

"Is it really all right or are you just saying that?"

"It's really all right."

Benjy laughed merrily. He truly was calm, strangely calm, as he walked through the snow in pyjama pants and bare feet.

"The truth is, old friend, I'm under the influence of a drug. I know that. I know it completely. And it knows me. So if I seem a bit bland, or even comical, I'm not bland or comical on the inside, I assure you. That's the funny thing."

He fell silent. "How *are* you?" I asked as I hurried him off the bridge and through the park.

"You won't believe me. It is funny, I know. But I'm trapped in here, screaming for help. Some of the time, at least. It keeps coming back to that. Only I can't get it out —everything comes out funny, excruciatingly funny! It's all such a good joke. But it's been two—three days, old friend. I'm scared I'll never get out of here!"

He started chuckling and I wanted to stop it. "Sure you will," I said. "Drugs wear off. I'm going to take you back and stick with you."

"Yes, yes do! Do stick with me! Please don't leave! Don't leave no matter what!"

Again he chuckled. "It won't do any good, you know. A fiber's torn in my head. Once the compartment is punctured, it can't be re-sealed. The leg is missing but you still feel it there. All the king's horses and all the king's men. . . . But don't go away from me, old friend. I need you on account of the fear."

We had started across the drive. Far up the line two slowly coming headlights glowed like moons through the snow's thick fabric. With a little cry, Benjy ran towards them, arms outstretched in supplication. I started after him but slipped and fell. The creeping car shuddered as its brakes clamped tight, its back wheels in a slow-motion skid to avoid the embrace of Benjy, who stood forlorn as the machine spun by him and plunged backwards into the park. There came an angry shout from the driver, and Benjy took off in panic up one of the intersecting streets.

I cut him off with a hard tackle. We lay in the gutter arguing whether to take him to the infirmary. He wanted to go, but I was wary of the Dean.

Benjy couldn't think about expulsion. "Why won't you let me?" he howled. "You're just acting, aren't you? None of you are real!"

"We'll go to the infirmary," I said.

"I've known of your planning for a long time," said Benjy. "All these years you've had me utterly in your power!"

"Except it's not so," I said.

"Replying right on cue," said Benjy.

The night nurse gave us towels and Benjy strode in to see the doctor wrapped in a toga-size special from neck to ankle. He stared in fascination as the doctor shined a little flashlight between his narrowed eyelids.

"You have the classic symptoms of someone who's taken a powerful stimulant," the doctor told Benjy. "What was it?"

"The Answer Drug."

"Do you know its technical name?"

"No."

"Do you know the possible consequences of ingestion?"

Benjy leaned against the wall and stared intently at an overhead lightbulb. The doctor sat scribbling on a record form.

"What *is* the technical name?" I asked. "What *are* the consequences, in your opinion?" The doctor went on scribbling.

He rose and walked to the window. "You exposed yourself to possible pneumonia," he announced to the night outside. He threw a tablet, or maybe a gumdrop, into his mouth. "Luckily you're not even chilled. I suggest bed rest. You'll find the effects soon wear away. Black coffee should help."

He gestured toward Benjy, who had slumped halfway down the wall, his jaw fallen slack as he stared at the bulb.

"Your friend is half asleep already. Can you be relied on to put him to bed? Or shall I call the university guard?"

I took a good look at the seamy face with its clever manly mustache, wondering how he put it all together. I guess it helped him to see kids like Benjy.

"Thanks for nothing," I said.

"If you don't respect professional treatment," the doctor said, "you're welcome to continue your own."

"I was thinking maybe some heroin—" I said, but I was cut off by Benjy.

"That won't be necessary," he said. "Thank you, doctor."

He shook hands firmly, turned and walked out in his towel like a Roman senator leaving the Forum.

One block down the street Benjy shoved me into a doorway. "Wavelengths! Pinwheels!" he cried. "All the energy's gotten loose from the lightbulb. Get down!

Duck! If we get caught in that red shift we'll disintegrate!"

I couldn't help laughing; Benjy was laughing himself as he cringed in the doorway, eyes popping.

"Your collar's too tight," I told him. "Loosen your tie."

Benjy groped inside his toga, and the next thing I knew he was on the ground again, strangling, his body twisting against the efforts of his own hands. He was yanking his striped rep tie as tight as it could knot, till he choked and writhed like a beached fish. When I finally unpried his fingers, he lay gasping and weeping.

"I haven't done anything," he whispered. "Really, I haven't done a thing. Cross my heart and hope to die!" He giggled. "But it doesn't matter. Whatever I say it's all the same!"

Despite the bombardment of light, I got Benjy safely back to the dorm on Mayflower Street. As we started up the steps Seymour's yellow roadcar pulled to the curb, driven by one of his black-jacketed technicians. There were two more in the back seat. By day they worked as electricians or mechanics in the big city; at night they were Seymour's. I told him he could come in without them. From inside the car I could feel them almost looking, feel the flickering of what normally would have been eyes, deep in the visored shaded jungle of their sockets.

"Why did you sell it to him?" I asked Seymour.

He shrugged. "I don't discriminate."

Yet Seymour could be helpful. He reached for Benjy unaffectedly and pressed him deep in his mouton coat, where Benjy groveled, giving grateful baby cooing. Between the two of us we walked him through the halls, shoving aside the student spectators, while Benjy kept safely buried in Seymour's rich fur.

He melted when we put him in the bathtub, mumbling of molecules of water coupling and decoupling down his leg in infinite series. He undulated enormous in satisfaction, spoke of water crackling in the pores of his skin, the round whole push of orgones.

I phoned Cathy, and by the time she got there we had Benjy in his warm flannel robe and blanketed in bed, where he lay with his eyes shut, rigidly still once more. Cathy wore her baggy tweed and in her milky black eyes that look of concern that made me flinch and backed Seymour clear into the next room.

Suddenly Benjy threw off his covers, held tight to his genitals and pressed his knees together, screaming for us to close the windows: his legs and arms had come loose and were sailing round the room, looking for a way out. Frantically he tried to stuff himself against the door-crack, where his right hand was creeping to ooze away from him forever.

To humor him I started a make-believe of retrieving and restoring his parts, but Cathy stopped me. She put her hand on Benjy's forehead and began to assure him that everything was where it should be. "But it *has* happened!" insisted Benjy between clenched teeth. "With a knife or many other ways!"

"Sssh." Cathy squeezed his hands and feet, gently rubbed his back, covered him up and tucked him in again.

Cathy went on talking, soothing, reassuring, with Benjy crying out from time to time. He did not really calm again till Seymour brought in a kaleidoscope. As in the bath, he fell into a crooning calmness, murmuring he was inside the tube, among mirrors and colored pebbles. He realized now he was himself a pebble, a pebble of pulsing color and vast quantities of light.

Cathy pulled me from the room. Her eyes were shining fiercely. "That Seymour person should be put in jail!"

"He doesn't force anyone," I said. "The Drug exists and people try it."

"Why do they!"

"Because it's supposed to give you an Answer. To yourself and everything."

Cathy shook her dark head in indignation.

"You mean people take it as a kind of . . . search? They think they're going to learn some special secret?"

"Why not?" You'd think she'd have known why people take it. "They have a right."

"Oh anybody has a right to do anything!" exclaimed my passionate Cathy. Her face was flushed with lovely anger.

"But it's stupid," she cried, "to fool around with your body. And to think it's going to change your life! What bullshit!"

"Why is it bullshit?" I said. I couldn't help pushing back against her. "Your life might be changed. Not by the Drug itself, but maybe just by taking it. So what if it's dangerous! That's just the point. You don't know what it means to take chances. And that's what it's all about!"

"That's what *what's* all about?" she screeched at me, grimacing as if she'd stepped in some unexpected dog-mes. She was ugly then; her face was distorted. And truly, she did not know what I was talking about. All she knew was woman-warmth, it seemed, with home and tea and diapers drying on the fire-dogs.

"I hear you whispering," shouted Benjy. "You're going to hurt me."

"Bad news!" moaned Seymour.

Benjy was bawling for me to come to him, his voice husky with fear and an odd undertone of pleasure. He told us he was inflating,. his body filling up with gas.

The room couldn't hold him—he would press against it, burst, and dissipate into the atmosphere.

"Like hell you will!" snapped Seymour. His hand fell like a slab of lard on Benjy's forehead. "You're the same size as ever, man. You're here in bed. Nothing's happening to you, believe me, and nothing will happen either!"

Benjy shut his eyes at once. Looking at me, Seymour continued: "That was a game you were playing to scare yourself. Play a groovy game now and feel groovy."

"I can't hear you," Benjy said quietly. "I'm in the process of compressing. I'm getting smaller . . . smaller than the finest grain. I am no longer of your sphere. I am inside you, all around you . . . everywhere."

Benjy lapsed from speech, his eyes shut very tight.

"Anything you say, babe," Seymour laughed. "Another game," he said to me, making no effort to whisper. "But a cooler game, dig?"

Five minutes passed uneventfully. Seymour seemed to have things under control. I didn't know how much I trusted him, but I did know he had a lot of experience, plus a motive, in this case, for bringing his customer through unharmed.

Cathy stood up. She'd forgotten: she had to get back home, change into her whites, and get to the hospital to check on her cultures. Her sitter would be waiting on the doorstep. And Huckleberry had been stashed with the woman downstairs, in full confidence that Mommy would come home and put him to bed.

She kissed me on the lips. On the landing she turned and called, "Be sure to phone me!" I watched her run down the stairs. I wanted to run after her and make her run with me through the streets like a couple of orangutangs.

Benjy still had his eyes shut. "Alex, I must see you alone," he whispered. When Seymour went out he snapped up his lids and spoke in that same super-calm that had come to him after our struggle on the bridge.

"It's still that way, old friend. I'm still not in command, you know. I don't want to be in here. The part that's me is smaller and smaller. I want something to pull me out. You've got to go for it, Alex. You can leave me with Seymour. I know he hates me but it's not a personal thing. I see that very clearly—and I can use it to hold on."

"Is there something that can pull you out?" I asked. "I thought you just had to wait."

"There is something," Benjy said. "You can get it from Dr. Tyrtan, old friend. It won't take you long."

Seymour waited in the livingroom, sitting at Benjy's littered desk, clicking off and on the flourescent tubelight.

"Is there an antidote?" I asked him.

He shrugged. "I guess so."

"If we could get him something," I said. "It might psych him right out of it. Two–three days he said: that's a long time."

"Shouldn't be that long," said Seymour. "He's had his trip already. What he's getting now is all aftereffect."

"Might it keep on going?"

"Might. I don't think so."

"Will you go to Dr. Tyrtan? Just to humor him?"

Seymour shook his head. "Most uncool, man."

"He has a right to it, don't you think? If he wants it."

"Why don't you go? Take my car. Dr. T. wants you, you know. Just take him up on his invitation. Say here I am, baby. Going to try it myself like the big boys!"

"Like Benjy?"

"You never know."

"I said no once. And seeing Benjy hasn't changed my mind."

"It hasn't gone away," said Seymour. It's still there waiting for you."

"I'd rather make it on my own."

Seymour giggled and smoothed his hair. "Beautiful!" he said. "Meanwhile what are you going to do? The man digs you. The company is charming, that I guarantee. When you came back it'll all be over. If not, you'll have something else for Benjy. The Lone Ranger with his silver bullet."

Benjy was calling me; he'd heard everything we'd said. "Go!" he begged. "See Tyrtan. He must have something. He'll give it to you, Alex! He was impressed with you. He wouldn't give it to Seymour, don't you see? He knows what Seymour is like. It has to be you!"

I didn't know whether to laugh or cry. The back of my neck was tingling. I couldn't keep my feet still while Seymour gave me directions to a place called Heavenly House, an hour's drive into the north woods.

"Be on the lookout!" Seymour sneered. "Sometimes they slip it up your fingernails!"

He was wheezing with maryjane laughter, having himself a ball. Well, why not? I thought. Between Benjy and me, it must have been a funny scene.

As I started down the stairs I thought I heard Benjy call my name. I turned back, but Seymour stuck his head out the door and waved me on, his face all-knowing, lips in silent form of "cool it."

5

THE DOWNFALL had stopped and I rode on into a cleanswept dark. The stars were high and cold and the city a bonnet of light in the black behind me. The roads lay empty, their yellow signals blinking to deserted intersections. Wisps of snow sucked windlessly across the roads and lay in shallow ridges on the fields.

I had gobbled a few milligrams of Dexadrine, but until it set in I had to concentrate fiercely on the churning snow and the coating of ice down where the roadtop lay. It had been weeks since I'd had a full night's sleep. Gradually I found there was no use fighting the wheel. I hit a maximum speed where I could safely skid and looped down that highway like a swan. With no other cars in view it was sweet sailing. I loosened my grip to a fine touch, driving my cunning sportscar like a painter, my mind easy-open to fields of rush and surge.

It was that last lecturer I was thinking of, the last of seven in the month of January, the last of the great darers, the word holders, the touring truth-bearers, the prophets and revolutionaries, of utmost danger to the established order because they were transformers, utterly, like us, like me at least, with nothing to lose and everything to gain. He had come back to celebrate the third anniversary of their firing him from the medical school, where he had onceuponatime distinguished himself in neurosurgery. No matter, he said, what they thought of him, so long as they let our generation grow older, without destruction or multilation in the wars of imperialists he prayed, and he would one day be reinstated—as chief of the Divinity School. He'd had grace enough to laugh, but already there were clerical converts, who could be seen afterwards, pressing his hand, hugging him close as all beheld.

I had expected Magus Tyrtan to be wild but his presence was cool. I hardly remembered anything but the voice, which held in its low thrilling tone a burr of modesty. With that voice he called it seemed to powers larger than himself which he could not even try to describe. He merely stood in the glow of his tiny light and let his one poor voice flow out into the darkened arena. The Answer Drug was beyond him, he admitted; he came to us as a simple enthusiast.

I resented the divineness of it, the adulation, the atmosphere, the humility too—and yet the man himself brought it off with humor. Afterwards Seymour introduced me, and as we stood there on the stage he said to my surprise he'd seen some of my poems in the lit magazine. We saw him an hour later in the coffeeshop, and this time he did not let go of my hand. He offered to turn me on—take me on a journey, as he put it. Remember, this was back in '64, before the flood of potentates and publicity. Dr. Tyrtan was just beginning to try his wings. Still, we knew him, all of us, he had begun with us and we were acutely aware of his coming. And for him actually to ask, with that most amazingly open forthrightness. . . . I knew that anyone else would have jumped—that is, anyone outside the system.

But I have a built-in perversity. I didn't want to. I just didn't want to. Tyrtan took it in stride—more: I think he really dug it. He only grinned and left a standing offer. "Sooner or later," he said, ". . . when the time is ripe." The others came and took him from our corner; yet he held my eye in grinning open recognition till they spun him out of sight.

The moon was silver bright with only a soft collar of haze as I turned from the main highway and ploughed cautiously up country roads. Luckily there had been cars: I found frozen mud ruts for my tires. I stuck to my slow grooves and drove on automatically up a winding slot between high hedges of evergreen, dense with weight of snow. Through occasional gaps I glimpsed farmhouses, barns, or ghostly fields covered smooth as prairies.

The first meeting with Tyrtan had set me up in a way that had nothing to do with him or what he said. Never mind why, I had that old feeling that the world was an apple I could take a great big bite of, if only I had eyes to see it hanging so ripe and ready, and guts to reach my arm up for it. Who if not me? I asked myself.

I believed, then if ever, in a new kind of society, beginning with personal realization and ending in a very basic change in what people are. There would be an end to national exploitation and selfishness, an end to the guilt-ridden family unit, an end to the monogamous rigidities in love manners and art. Laughing our fool heads off, we would stamp out middle-class smugness, dullness, sameness and complacency. We would abolish nations and live in spontaneous groups, body to body, monkey kings, suffusing every movement, every act, every human gesture with a wild true harmony, a music of the senses hitherto heard only in our imaginations.

You can see why two days after Tyrtan I had fallen very low again. It was the contrast, I thought. You could feel it but you couldn't live it—I couldn't, at least. The society was just too much, you couldn't get away from it. The others absolutely *would not* be free! And until they were my simplest invitation would be seen as seduction, my most natural reaching out as rape.

So I had it all worked out. The only trouble was that people existed—like Dr. Tyrtan or the Blonde Star or the artists and writers you can read about—who were free anyway, maybe, because of what they were or what they knew or how they went about it. Which left me in dread of a possible lacking inside me—a hole I could never find and never fill.

It had gotten worse in the drearest of all exam months, this goddamn February, this bad taste to be expunged from the passages. But as my mood slipped the perversity came happily to surface. The more I screwed it up with people the more I said to myself I don't need them anyway. There was nothing I needed; I had more, I said, and I'd see it through, blah blah.

I pulled up before long at the looming stone gatehouse Seymour had spoken of. The archway beneath was closed off by metal pickets; beyond that, a moonless blackness. High in the gatehouse burnt a single light; I gave a short toot on my horn. No one came: I felt myself seen without seeing. I got out and swung the heavy gate with my shoulder, my footsteps echoing like heavy blows deep within the grounds.

For a mile my car crept slowly in a tunnel cut through an overarching hedge, till I drove round a bend and caught sight of a gap where moonlight poured through. I drove out onto a little bridge, and stopped. Below a lake lay frozen, fringed with dark bare trees. Before me a vast estate in patches of light and shadow, with electric stabbings from the narrow windows of outbuildings and a sheath of yellow fanning up from behind a thick grove. I parked my car in a clearing near four others and went on foot up a winding path among the trees.

High horns mew out, piercing me, not five yards from where I freeze! Hi-fi somewhere; I could see the outline of a speaker. Indian music raving from the trees. Tear your mind out by the roots, nearly, if that's your pleasure and why not? Back on the path I take the brunt of a treestump across my thighs. Top of the stump hollowed out; my hand gropes and comes up with doll figure. Turn it this way and that. Ugly creature: matted blond hair, thick trunk like mine. Museum warrior doll, put it to cheek but a dot of pain, a pricking on my lips. Pin through the head, nothing too corny. I draw the pin and drop the doll back in the woodslime of its pit.

Another speaker—same music only different. And now a mansion through the trees, sprawling out at the base of a hill, many lights in great and small windows. I make my way plodding up the path, conscious of other objects in the trees: tinkle chimes, charms, stuffed elves and goblins. I come on like Snow White up the long snow-trampled front lawn, old wood and stone looming four stories above me, topped with turrets and balconies against the moon.

Electricity buffeting from all sides, marching symphonic and free new jazz blast slicing up the oriental. Also the murmur and chant of separate quiet voices from above and beyond unwavering as I stomp across the broad-planked porch. At the oaken door I pause and try to peer through glowing ruby sidepanels. Should I grab the jamb and hoist to the blue pale fanlight?

Benjy, Benjy, waiting to get out. Strongly I knock, and the door is opened by a young woman with soft doe eyes.

"Welcome," she says. She hands me a flower.

"Open your hand," she says quietly.

6

THE LIGHT CAME from behind her, tracing a soft halo about her high-piled hair. "Please come in." She stepped back lithely—relaxed, yet finely alert.

"You had better take off your shoes," she said.

I preferred to slosh them on the doormat.

She turned to fetch Dr. Tyrtan and I had a glimpse of her soft heart-shape held gently in jeans worn to a tissue-white smoothness. "Wait a minute," I said. "I have to know your name."

"My name?" she said. "Nina." She did not smile.

"Alex Randall," I said.

"I know."

And she was off, her slim calves twinkling in high kid boots.

I stood alone in the hallway, purple gentian jammed in my pantstop. Near me an elephant's-foot umbrella-stand guarded a great wooden wardrobe jammed with jackets, hat, gloves and boots spilling over. Expensive skis and ski-poles lay across the top; tinted goggles and an old-war leather flying cap hung from the braided cornerposts. Further on the hall branched into corridors from which voices and music drifted louder than before. I entered a passageway and stopped at the sight of a rifle on its stock in the corner.

Retreating to the threshold I discovered a curious

door hung with layers of bamboo. I stuck my arms in and found myself grappling with layer after layer so thick that I could not see the room beyond. The strips were twined about my neck; I yanked and flailed—as heavy footfalls sounded in the corridor behind! My first slip: I wrenched free, fell clumsily backwards. A hulk loomed, arms-crossed, staring down at me from beneath black shaggy eyebrows, shaved head blotting out the light. Near me two army boots were planted.

"I'd like to see Dr. Tyrtan," I said, scrambling up.

The giant smiled contemptuously. A luminous jewel hung like a drop of water from his left earlobe. We stood there, tooth to eyeball. I had the feeling he might speak, if only I gave the sacred sign. Yank twice on the jewelry, touch mustache tips to eyebrows?

"I have a secret whistling mirror ring," I told him.

Nina was back. She grabbed a single strand of the curtain and pivoted the whole thicket cleanly away, motioning for me to enter. I did, and the bamboo snapped in place behind me.

"Aha!" I cried. If I were a prisoner I would skulk about and pry into everything. What I saw was a country-squire study, pine-paneled with laden bookshelves covering two walls. By the light of large parchment lamps I saw writing cabinets with leather surfaces and whalelike leather armchairs wallowing on Persian carpets. No turntable in sight, but the familiar voice of Fats Waller eased from a recessed speaker. I went toward it, as who wouldn't, and discovered Dr. Tyrtan deep in one of the armchairs.

"Hello," he said pleasantly, and I said "Hi."

He looked at me with frank untroubled gaze, lounging with one leg up and an open book in his lap. He looked younger than he was, could have passed for thirty with his freckled face unlined and red hair curling high above his domed forehead. He had scarlet lips, scarcely any eyebrows, and sky blue eyes slightly bulging. Like me, he wore slacks and a crew sweater.

"Can I help you?" he said.

"I guess you don't remember me," I began.

"Oh, but I do, Alex."

He did!

"Sit down," he said.

We looked at each other for one long moment. "Well," he said.

"A friend of mine flipped out on the Answer Drug," I said quickly. "Is there anything you can give me to pull him back?"

He cocked his head a little sadly.

"I'm sorry to hear that. But why did you come to me?"

"Because the person who sold him the Drug is a friend of yours. Seymour."

He gave no sign.

"Seymour Simon."

He nodded.

"And the Drug must have come from you!"

He looked away grinning as if not to embarrass me.

"You know better than that," he said. "If you think I'm supplying the black market, why didn't you bring the police, start up the law machine?"

"That's not my way."

"Not even for your friend?"

I was baffled. A minute passed. Tyrtan still sat with head averted, humming mildly to Fats Waller.

"I didn't size it up like that," I said. "I thought you'd want to help."

Tyrtan strolled to the French windows, thoughtfully fingered a silk-backed curtain.

"Tell me about your friend," he said.

Pacing his Persian, I told him the sad story of Benjy, talking too much, telling too much, yet spewing it out in little pieces impossible to pull together. No one listening could have seen Benjy as I still see him, in all his possibilities. Tyrtan at last held up his hand to stop me.

"It's pitiable," he said softly, "truly pitiable."

"Yes."

"It's mostly the family, isn't it?"

"They have one of the oldest investment houses in America. Really dig him, too, give him everything he wants. But nothing to live for."

"His father is something of a playboy, I believe," mused Dr. Tyrtan. "Kind of like my old man. He owns an airline, you know. Used to have my own private plane to fly friends to the Riviera. Then I became a doctor, very distinguished business. Father makes a pile and son heals the sick. The old man doesn't know what to think since I changed my way of life. Every once in a while he tries the broken-heart routine. But deep down he's too hip to himself. In the middle of every scene he breaks up laughing."

"It's a kind of pattern," I said. "My own father made his money the hard way. I can respect that. But how do you go on from there?"

Tyrtan flopped back in his chair. "Let's sit down and talk more beautifully," he said. "Oh what a day this has been!" He ran his hand through his springy hair. "Manifestations without end!"

"But what do we do about Benjy, I mean now?"

"Oh there's nothing, nothing new," sighed Tyrtan. "I doubt very much your friend is in real danger. That aspect of the Drug has been exaggerated by panicked puritans. Very soon now he'll loosen his grip, pass through his hell and fall asleep. When he wakes he will be born into . . . something else. Or more likely he'll do his best to carry on exactly as before. The mind is a wonderful thing! I take it he's now in his own bed, and Seymour Simon is sitting up with him?"

"Yes."

"Then he'll come through all right. Seymour is an adequate guide."

"Unless he sends Benjy out the window, just for a gas!"

Tyrtan laughed right in my face. "You think so?"

I nodded, stupidly grim.

"Then why did you leave your friend with him?"

"And why did you pass out drugs to him?"

Tyrtan rose, unruffled, and moved towards the curtain where I had entered.

"Going to get your goon?" I called after him.

Tyrtan shook his head with that grin again.

"You're referring to one of the most intelligent people I know. If I want him, incidentally, I can signal any time as simply as this."

He fiddled at a panel and the music stopped. A minute later Quentin appeared with two sandwiches and two bottles of Danish beer on an incongruous metal saloon tray.

"Just a servant then?" I needled.

"All of us have what you might call our tribal duties. Tomorrow I'll be serving him."

I reached for a sandwich and bit down on a thick slab of sugar-cured ham between leaves of fresh rye. But I noticed that Tyrtan had a thinner sandwich.

"I don't eat flesh of any sort," he explained. "But I never impose. And you look so thoroughly carniverous!"

I liked that.

"Impose, hell! I thought you were trying to poison me!"

"I may yet!"

For the first time we laughed together, and washed down our sandwiches with first-class beer.

I put my feet up on a hassock.

"What if Benjy really does go round the bend? People do, don't they? I've read about them."

"But have you ever known a case personally?"

"I've known people who've known people."

Tyrtan glanced up happily from under his outcrop of forehead.

"I don't have to say anything, do I Alex? But just for the record, because you'll be thinking about this later: in five years of experimenting, I have not seen one single case of so-called insanity. Insanity is a game that can't be played without cooperation. All that's required to forestall it is the presence of a loving, thoughtful person."

"Like Seymour!"

"Seymour will do. You're not so responsible yourself."

I began to pace again, bothered by the feeling there was more for me to say. But I couldn't think what; he had me dangling.

"You're in an interesting position, Alex. You might as well relax and look around you."

Tyrtan had his feet up and had taken a cigarette from a little ceramic pot. He offered me one and I declined. He shrugged genially and went on smoking, lowering his heavy eyelids with each drag.

"Why do they say it if it isn't so?"

"Say what?"

"That your drug flips people out."

"Well it does! It makes them see things differently. And the society doesn't like that. It has its interests to protect. But I don't have to tell you about that."

"Not about that, no . . ."

But about what? What was the point of it?

"It's pretty complicated," said Tyrtan patiently.

I stopped, out of gas. Tyrtan continued to stare mildly, as if waiting for some sign.

"What if I wanted to take you up?" I said quickly. "Myself. Now."

Tyrtan slowly smiled. "Oh," he said. I felt my foolish stomach clutch, my face was flushing. "I see what you mean," he said.

And then said nothing while I waited.

He was examining his cigarette. He turned it in his long white fingers. Around one of the fingers wound a silver ring with a translucent red stone twisted into its center.

"But you know we never give drugs here. I didn't mean here."

"You mean you never give drugs to outsiders?"

"No. We give no drugs. It's against the law you know."

"Who you kidden?" I said.

He looked up sharply.

"You know, you're a beautiful person, Alex. I'm getting beautiful signals on your wavelength."

"No static?" I tried to slip in.

"—Does that upset you?" Suddenly he giggled, like any pothead but way beyond, I wasn't prepared for it, the high-pitched manic note without the slightest inhibition.

"I used to dig the way you played football," he said. "The abandon. I picked up signals way back then."

"You don't look like much of an athlete," I mumbled.

"I do a little flying. In fact, I think of myself as a flight instructor." Again the giggle. "Besides, the goal of any game is ecstasy."

"I don't know what you're talking about," I said.

"Yes you do," he said.

"Anyway I had to quit that scene—" I began, turning away as he came near. But he cut me off with a hand on my shoulder.

"Later," he said; "don't talk about it. Perhaps you'd like to see the grounds."

Dr. Tyrtan pulled on a pair of sleek riding boots and slipped a cablestitch sweater over his head.

"Don't you need a coat?" I said. He only smiled, I winced, and out the back door we went and up between the stable and the guest house. Back in the main house the voices were going strong; candles flickered, colored lights pulsed in upper windows.

We walked up a pathway into a clump of woods, turned sharply down where the path forked, and came out presently on a road running perpendicular to the main road. There were houses here and there along this road, formerly the cottages of tenant farmers and groundskeepers, now used mainly, as Tyrtan explained, for "visiting artists."

We came to the parking lot where I'd left Seymour's car. The moon was low, hidden behind a silver cloud. Against the cloud, very near, leaned what looked to me like a wooden fire tower.

"Funny," I said. "I must have driven right by without seeing it."

"There's always something you overlook," said Tyrtan a little absently. He glanced up slyly as if he'd said something clever.

"Could I climb up?" I asked. "I always like to climb things."

"I'm afraid not. Someone's up there right now."

"Oh that's all right," I said, setting my foot on the

bottom rung. In a second I would pull up powerfully and he would have to stop me or come after.

But he grabbed my arm right away. "Sorry, no," he said. "All right for you, but not for him. One of us is always up there you know, watching over us, representing the whole community. We never interrupt him, except at sunrise or sunset when the power is changed."

"The power? Is it a ghost up there or a human being?"

"I won't interfere with your distinction-making," Tyrtan said. "Our watch tonight is the son of the gentleman who owns this estate. Jacky!" he called.

The tower remained dark and silent. "No one home," I said.

"Wait."

A white hand appeared; it fluttered like a handkerchief. A radiant voice sang hello.

"Just passing by," called Dr. Tyrtan.

"Travelers, pass on," the voice sang. "The universe has no opposite."

"Well that's a relief," I said.

I began laughing and Tyrtan laughed too. Silvery laughter floated from the top of the tower. A head appeared. "Hail to thee, laughing pilgrim. Seek ye the light, beware of fire."

"Okay!" I cried. "It's a deal!"

The head had vanished and the moon thrown off its wisp of cloud.

"More! More!" I shouted, but my words echoed back to me unanswered.

I turned towards the car. "Thanks for the sandwich," I said.

"Complete the circle with me," said Tyrtan. "And see what you will see."

"I've seen a lot already."

"See more!"

He strode on and I hurried after. See more! I never say no to that.

Leaning half forward, Tyrtan walked on at a fast clip, his face set, his fair cheeks mottled by the cold. Without a glance in my direction he plunged off the path and into a field of deep snow that lay off the left wing of the house. The ground sloped upward, gradually leveling to what must have been, in summer, a fine lawn terrace for croquet. Under the free full moon it shimmered now in virgin snow.

Suddenly Tyrtan clutched my wrist. "Look!"

Back from the shadow of the house a form came floating pale as a spirit. Despite myself I shivered.

The figure spun slowly, throwing up blossoms of translucence; turning, veering, gliding closer. My bones glowing, I made her for a girl, unbelievable, dancing barefoot on the lawn beneath the moon, dressed merely in a gown of filmstuff.

She stopped, poised: her moon-silvered hair settled like a cloud. She had seen us.

Tyrtan nudged me. "Her name is Amber. Go ahead —touch her."

As in a dream I stepped across the space of intervening snow. The girl waited wide-eyed, my enchanted creature. She was too beautiful. "Amber!" Lovingly she smiled. I stretched out to caress the softness of her thick falling hair and she swayed her neck and lay her cheek upon my hand. For a moment nothing moved in the whole world. Time itself had jammed I thought in one bold thrust of freedom.

Then, with a little cry, she bit my hand and sprang back laughing. When I stepped after she went into a violent bump and grind. I dared not touch her. I stood frozen, moronically rubbing my palm-flesh where it tingled yet from the nip of her snowy teeth.

Footstomps impinged upon my hearing. A bear-man lumbered through the snow, moonface dully shining, glass eyes reflecting blankly in a heap of dullgloss fur. It was Seymour the Serene, unmistakably, in his mouton coat with the hood up. He talked in undertones to Dr. Tyrtan. I walked across to them, escaping.

Seymour only nodded.

"Your friend Benjy has come out the other side," announced Dr. Tyrtan. "He's sleeping like a baby."

"That right?" I asked Seymour.

He nodded again, as if irritated.

"He won't wake for many hours yet," said Dr. Tyrtan. "It's as I told you. Appearances mean nothing. Things are never as they seem."

With a grunt Seymour lunged on past us. And damned if the girl wasn't posed again and waiting! As Seymour plodded towards her she reached down langourously and rubbed her thigh, shook her breasts, slid the filmy slick stuff on her belly—in a touching conception of burlesque. Seymour put an arm about her, enveloping her in fur. He put his thick lips to her ear, kissing and whispering, gesturing towards me so that Amber giggled and I saw the tip of her tonque flick teasingly across her teeth.

"You'd better get out of the cold, my cutlet," called Dr. Tyrtan. Seymour steered the girl away. "Remarkable child," said Tyrtan. "She's been into quite a bit for sixteen years old. I think you'll find that everyone here is a most unusual person."

"Will I?"

"I trust you'll stay with us," said Tyrtan smoothly, "now that there's no emergency to send you rushing back. You must be terribly tired."

It was, after all, nearly morning. As Tyrtan spoke I felt the strength for a return trip sap from me. My legs were heavy from all-night stumping, first in town with Benjy, now out in the country, where the snow had drifted even higher. I followed almost meekly toward the massive house.

"Just one question," I said. "Must I come as a pilgrim? Whatever that is? Or can I just find a bed and sleep?"

"Alex, something's disturbing you, isn't it?" Dr. Tyrtan stopped and looked at me full face with brow-furrow of deep concern. "I get distress signals on your wavelength. You're a very strong person, I know, but somewhere inside I hear a little boy crying in a locked room."

"So I *am* a pilgrim, like it or not!"

"That's up to you," said Tyrtan. But still he peered at me, expecting.

"I won't be anything," I said.

He shrugged and we went on, crossed a drive which wound alongside the house, ducked through some shrubbery and into a side door. I followed him up a narrow passageway set with dark storerooms and all at once emerged into a brightly lit manorial kitchen, where piercing bebop blared from a six-foot speaker. A household of faces crowded forth to press against their leader. I'd had enough, tried to edge to the far side of a heavy old iron stove where a Negro cook with a cloth on her head was ladling out cocoa. I remember too a ceiling-rack with pots and cooking tools hanging down, some oaken counters with cups and plates unwashed, a fireplace with dogs basking on raised hearthstones—and the people. They were babbling, smiling, all knowing one another. I didn't see the young woman Nina, nor Seymour and Amber. Dr. Tyrtan was sitting down and had not thought to introduce me. In an alcove I saw a massive oaken table with something soft on it which I could quite naturally slip aside to look at. I stroked it, pretending to be absorbed. But my hand came back wet and I shuddered, having fondled the carcass of a newly-killed deer.

Furtively I got a napkin; Tyrtan noticed me then and spoke my name. The faces turned in acknowledgment, curious but reserved, politely placing me outside. I didn't have the energy; I was exhausted. Tyrtan got the cook to lead me upstairs and off to a far wing, where I slept on a mattress in a room soft with draperies hung from walls and ceiling.

I was so tired I didn't bother to look. Yet once I lay down behind the closed door I couldn't sleep; I twitched at every noise, voice, step. Was it strangeness only or was I stupidly afraid? I got up and pressed against the tapestries, to make sure solid walls were there. What good did it do? Remembering Amber, I conjured up at last my recourse, my Blonde Star, the Only One, dead in fact but forever accessible to my trained imagination, where I lay, so proud, able to slow down camera, very certain, perfect flesh, the firmness of it, inch by inch, no sagging no blemish, while moist lips part for more and more more. . . .

7

Having come down from the tower, Jacky Mayflower was simultaneously conducting a tour of the house and telling me the story of his life. On his vacations from prep school he had gone on six separate African safaris. Once he had gotten deathly sick in the jungle, and in mosquito delirium came his first intimations of the beyond. "But I kept it to myself, you know? One doesn't talk about such things among the Mayflowers. Reminds them right away of my Uncle who had a thing on spiritualists and spent thirty years seeking out one after another. Finally he became an Hasidic Jew, converted—yomica, earlocks, the whole bit. A real soul-brother. I was forbidden to talk to him but there was a time when every afternoon I was in New York, supposedly to skate or go to museums, I'd snatch the D train down to East Broadway to watch him through a basement window read the cabala. They have these reading rooms, you know? I waited on that sidewalk hours and hours, but he never looked up and never came out for air."

"You could meet him now," I said. "You could go wherever he lives!"

"Naw," said Jacky. "He died some strange way while I was still a kid. The Hasidics refused even to bury him. He's dug in here somewhere on the grounds. None of the family were allowed to come—health board brought him out and put our servants through a whole process."

Mayflower twitched back his mop of walnut hair, a plump little squire in double-breasted blazer, silk polka-dot shirt and flowery cravat. Up dusky corridors he led me, striding along on blocky legs and wellfleshed feet in walking shoes handcarved in Sussex. We swung past chiseled balustrades and climbed up odd-angled staircases, me tripping along behind him and peering into rooms left trustingly open.

"Look in," urged Jacky, "go ahead. We have no hangups on privacy."

Most of the rooms were maid-servant small with sparse furnishings: a flimsy mattress on the floor, strewn clothing, brokendown armchairs sprinkled with pipes, candles, incense burners. Always though there was paint on the walls in wild irridescent patterns, or newsprint collage, or scraps of textured fabric. And sometimes I found sumptuous decorations à la fashion mag French Quarter, and in one room silks, furs, and antiques—including an empty crib.

Jacky went on talking, his dark eyes wide and peculiarly intent. He had once gone to the same University as myself, but quit after three years of class-taking and one year of credits. "I quit because I learned who I was," he told me. "That's what you go for, isn't it?"

"Yeah," I said, "I guess." Should I get into it? "Who *are* you anyway?" I asked instead.

"Only the momentary center of myself," he replied cheerfully. "Of course that center includes an infinity of possible ecstasies."

"That's nice," I said.

"It is," he agreed. "But man, I'm telling you, I went through some changes till I met Dr. Tyrtan."

"—And he saved you?"

"Oh no man. I read Dr. T's religious and scientific writings the way I read a modern novel. You look for art in these things, a style of apprehending. I'm not looking for personal salvation at this point. But there's a whole new way of thinking I fell into. You can't get away from it, it's evolving now everywhere, wherever there are young people. Thought isn't linear anymore; it's not just a matter of ABC."

We passed a cavernous library, where high carved windows stretched to the overcast day. In an enclave of soft old couches sat men and women in subdued conversation, whispering and blowing tender smoke to a tinkle plinkle of sorrowful folk rock. They nodded, I nodded. Quentin rose from among them to adjust the record controls, his bald dome placid in dull daylight shine. He wore neat slacks and an open-necked sportshirt with lead cross dangling down, half-waving to Jacky as cordial as a psychotherapist.

After college Jacky bought himself a coffeehouse on the Lower East Side, as close as possible to the reading room of his ex-Uncle. Soon he brought in young jazz musicians who had abandoned rhythm form tone technique in favor of the sounds that came to them."Absolute freedom, that's where it's at," explained Jacky. "All the way back from Africa. Sheer terror to the power structure."

"Like your relatives?"

"Not at all, man. They wouldn't think of interfering. In fact they dig my black friends at their cocktail parties. Now they want Dr. Tyrtan very bad, baby, they'd cream in their linens if he walked in. They're hypocrites and lushes my people but at least they're not square."

High in a turret we passed a heavy door to which

a cardboard key had been pasted, labeled "The Key to Mine Heart—For Dr. T."

"That's Gordion's room. Incredibly talented musician you know but he came here a hopeless junkie."

"Does he play now?"

Mayflower shook his head. "Not necessary."

Just for kicks Jacky had started a small record business.

"Teens began to happen about that time. Especially British teens. The now things, you dig, not just for like the Junior prom but cosmopolitan, for all of us."

Jacky quickly signed up a few authentic talents and proceeded, he said, "to bring folk into the mainstream. I was the guy who started all that. I don't give a damn if I ever get the recognition, but it's true, it's a fact."

After that he opened a combination discotheque-boutique-beauty parlor-film center-kinetic art gallery.

We had traversed the house from one wing to the other, descended a back staircase and filed through the great kitchen. Seeing a long side-room off the main hall where sliding doors stood open, I ventured inside; but pulled up quickly at the sight of so many silent squatters. This was the meditation room, Jacky whispered: the family group sat cross-legged on mattresses and prayer-rugs, head bowed in silent thought. Tyrtan sat on a special rug in the center, woven by tooth no doubt from fleece of Himalayan albino llamas.

No one looked. "Is that Nina—way in back?" I whispered. She wore huge impenetrable shades.

"Might be Noni," said Mayflower. "They're identical birds."

And there was Amber, sitting close to Seymour, all wound up in short skirt and striped tights and jersey, oblivious, meditating with all her might. Seymour looked at me coldly, no expression. But I loved to see the slight flush of the girl's face, the pure rose blood beneath her blonde earlocks. Tyrtan glanced up, saw me and broke out his evil grin, eyes flashing. Nervously I looked away —couldn't take that—to the carved decorations paneling the wall, which flickered like the surface of a dark soup as it bounced reflections from the smoulder of the fire. Opposite the mammoth fireplace a ballet mirror stretched the length of the far wall, doubling the haze which rose from scattered incense sticks. High on a side wall tiny square windows held patches of grey morning. Jacky nudged me to look up: to an elaborate mandala painted on the ceiling, wherein a circle of fragile stalks receded concentrically, waving me in among them. Pleasant to rest the eye . . . I tilt my head this way and that. . . .

Tyrtan is murmuring—where did he begin?—eyes closed off in deep engrossment of ". . . the Void unobstructed: shining, thrilling, blissful diamond Buddha being. . . ."

I shudder. "Let's get out of here."

"You're welcome to stay," my guide assures me.

But I went off and he followed, watching me in a tender smugness which I tried to break by asking the current state of his enterprise.

"All sold now," he said. "I think they closed it down. But for a while there we had space in all the media every day. There were lines around the block from the moment school let out each afternoon. I could have had much power. . . ." He rubbed his pudgy knuckles.

"But at the time I was getting more and more involved with Dr. Tyrtan and the Answer Drug. At first he sought me out. He dug the total scene I'd put together. Right away he saw me as this terrific catalyst. He gave me confidence to acknowledge my full creativity. Creativity, funny concept: it has to be redefined you know to include the sixth sense for coordinating media. It's no good just to get there first: you have to know how to send out word."

It was hard to listen precisely or take in particulars of passing rooms. More than any single phrase or object the labyrinthine enormity of the house itself overwhelmed me; I wandered drunk with the motion of twisting corridors, reeling in pocketed light of glossy lacquered walls and reflecting tiles, writhing in the whirl of moldings which stretched like vines along the crossings of planes repeating buds and grapes and birds and flowers infinitely varying past door after door after door.

At last I clutched at a siding, stopped to breathe, and stumbled into a lounge where two whipslender models in men's suits and capes, snapbrim hats and riding boots, looked up from their leopard couch with charcoaled glares. Beneath them a young girl lay supine, short skirt curling over tender fatted thighs, peering up grimly into a cluster of lightbulbs wired to click off and on in changing combinations. "Are you all right?" I blurted, but one of her coachmen half rose with gloved hand tight on her riding stock and Jacky pulled me away. The kittengirl had not moved, not even blinked.

"Are *you* all right?" said Jacky.

"I'd like a coke or something," I said.

He led me down another flight of stairs.

It's a funny thing, Alex," he said. "You learn to put it all in perspective. I guess in the final analysis I've been successful in wordly terms. Then too my family's holdings gave me a head start, I don't deny that. I was brought up to water at the mouth for every good thing you could get in this world, and I got 'em. But I was working on the striving-acquisitive model. And I found I wasn't happy, I had to have something more—"

"Just like my old man," I said.

"Well turn him on!"

"If I could only turn him off!"

"Hip old man," shrugged Jacky.

I got my coke from a machine in a long burlaped room labeled Publicity Office. Tacked to the burlap were articles, clippings and photographs of Dr. Tyrtan—lecturing in college amphitheatres, on pilgrimage by the Ganges, with policemen or in court. In many photos Tyrtan's thick eyelids were half-lowered, the eyes themselves supernaturally large and unfocused—and on these someone had taken a crayon and outlined the eyes in circles of blue.

The room was cluttered with typewriters, papers, opened letters, choked ashtrays, vacant coke-bottles. An adding-machine sat on a steel filing-cabinet, near a thuggish old black safe. On the safe, a stack of pamphlets with irridescent titles: "Two Institutions."

"Report on two funny farms?" I asked, wincing at my own language.

"Not exactly!" Mayflower chuckled. He was very happy and kept batting his glossy eyes at me. "The two institutions are Death and Marriage. We're starting two centers, you know? Look—applications!"

He threw a pile of white sheets up in the air, closing his eyes in pleasure as they came splashing down on his upturned face.

"A couple dozen come in every week. Costs ten bucks to apply, then two hundred each seven days if you're accepted."

"You mean for the Drug?"

Jacky shook his head. "Narcotics bulls come down on us."

"Then what's the point? What's a Center for Death?"

He shrugged so happily. "A real Sunday school,"

he said slowly, "where you learn techniques . . . to make death . . . a meaningful experience."

"The new thing," I said.

"We've given the Drug to a woman who had a terminal case of stomach cancer," said Jacky blandly as he sorted press releases. "Profound effect man! For X amount of days that woman was tranquil and composed. And when the pain returned, she could bear it."

"Did she know she was dying?"

Jacky smiled. "Her conception of death . . . was altered."

"Then death didn't bother her?"

"Should it have?"

Jacky coyly waited. I wanted him to tell more, but he waited for the answer to his marvelous question. I decided to tell a story.

"I watched my Uncle Walter die of stomach cancer. The pain was excruciating. At times he was nothing but a bundle of sticks thrashing about a grotesquely knotted belly. You know I think my father would have killed him—killed his own brother—if they hadn't taken him away, finally, to the state hospital. But when they got him there he wouldn't take their medicine. They couldn't get it in till the pain completely overcame him."

"Playing the hero?" Jacky chuckled.

"He *was* a hero! He knew he was dying and he hated it, but he said he'd be goddamned if he'd die a fool!"

Jacky casually shuffled his papers while inwardly I cursed myself. The need, the need! The truth was lost because I'd had to push it out and twist it.

Jacky turned his face up and threw his mop back happily.

"I really dig your uncle," he said. "What did he do?"

"Nothing much. He had a store."

Jacky sighed. "I've cut down myself, cut down quite a bit." I fingered the photographs, looking back into Tyrtan's strange whirlpool eyes, which seemed not to look out at all but only to suck back on themselves.

"My only outside activity," continued Jacky, "is an exclusive contract with a group called The Seven Sikhs from Calcutta." He turned to me glowing. "Something else, man! A year from now they'll be household words of the underground. In a way they're beyond even drugs, you'd dig that, Alex, they have that purity scene going for them in the true Asian sense. Even to what you'd call a fanatic degree, slashing and so on, I mean completely untouched by Anglo-Saxon inhibitions. . . ."

A gong sounded. "What's that?"

"End of meditation. Ablutions now, then lunch."

"Not that I'm contemptuous of money," Jacky warned me on our way downstairs. "I burned, literally burned, a thousand dollar bill one day last month. And I got out of that bag. I know what money symbolizes. To be really groovy in times like these you need a lot of money. Without it you can't really simplify. Which I have done to a dramatic degree. I'm completely attuned now to the vibrations emerging from all these non-white tradition cultures. It extends even to your diet. After a while you see right through your social commitments. You completely drop the ironic mask of the Western intellectual. The only things that matter are your internal neurological explorations. And it's only then, ironically, you begin to take your place in history."

By this time we were among the others and sat down to simple lunch. Dr. Tyrtan headed a table of quiet, frugal eaters to whom he handed loaves of acorn bread, paper plates of American cheese, a Mayan ritual bowl full of popcorn and a crocker pitcher of grape Koolaid.

I ate uneasily at first. Amber watched too closely. I thought I would cut out after lunch. I might take Seymour's car, but he was absent from the lunch table. Benjy's bike would do—Seymour had brought it out. The place was creeping up on me. The point was lost without the Drug.

"Did you phone your friend?"

I glanced up and saw that Tyrtan was talking to me. He had put on a leather pilot's cap; a photographer flashed a flashgun. I wanted to laugh but he was too serious and straight.

"I will," I said. "I figured he'd still be sleeping."

Tyrtan nodded briskly and the meal went on. People coming, going, violins seeping from the speaker above. A reporter from EAT magazine was interviewing Dr. T., and a lady sociologist was soaking it up on her wrist-watch tape recorder.

Except for Amber silently watching me eat and putting more food on my plate, the inhabitants ignored us visitors. To my left a young boy was holding forth on the development of a famous rock 'n' roll group. He wore a white smooth-haired turtleneck which set off his creamy beardless face and soft black hair. "Coolness for them creates a fantastic kind of involvement—"

"Johnnie eat your soup, your soup is cold," interrupted Amber. But Johnnie went on lecturing to the table at large, where the others ate with their heads down, picking them up only to wink or exchange some quick comment.

"They're into something entirely new. And it's interesting, it's extraordinarily interesting . . ."

The sociologist was watching him, nodding mouth open as she adjusted her tape controls with knobby middle-aged fingers.

"They're authentic," she confirmed with a heavy

blink and a nod. Johnnie didn't so much as glance at her. "It's a matter of extreme grace," he went on. "Whatever they do they never lose their almost classical poise."

"Well I think in general," said the sociologist, "the mod movement in Great Britain is the most hopeful cultural development in the last hundred years, in the West that is. All these young people just *vomiting up centuries* of puritanism!"

"Great vomiters us puritans," I mumbled.

Amber lightly stroked the nape of my neck. Across the table a man looked up at the sociologist and put his hand over his mouth. His round head stuck up from his sticklike body like a lollypop. I recognized Nelson Rosenberg, now making a definite grimace of nausea, once known in our college town as a brilliant grad student in Chemistry.

"Hi," I began, pitching my voice up to carry across the table. Rosenberg merely frowned and picked at his food like a childrens camper.

I got up from the table and went to a pay phone on the wall in the foyer. I dialed my own number back at the dormitory. No answer. The phone buzzed twenty times. I hung up and dialed again. Benjy was still asleep; he slept like a stone, inviolable. Or he might be spending the day in the bathtub, reading an old Sunday newspaper. Or flown to Jamaica to dance the Monkey, or to L.A. or Vegas. He sometimes flew far in the reborn moods which followed his depressions. Nonetheless I held the receiver and listened to my own phone ring and ring, giving extra time, giving yet a little more time, till Nina walked on by.

Silent as a doe in her calfskin moccasins, soft sweatshirt and smooth bluejean shorts, she leaned her silken thighs against the table and calmly began to assemble little cheese and cracker sandwiches.

I sat down next to her, but she took no notice. I leaned back in my chair for a better look just as Dr. Tyrtan, sitting on the other side, laid his hand upon the curve of her buttocks, and without looking rubbed up and down in affection as he ate his buttered bread and she her crackers. Slowly I let my chair down. Beneath Johnnie's talk I could hear Nina (or Noni?) speaking quietly to Tyrtan, asking him to take the grocery list when he drove to town. And Tyrtan's low voice in reply.

I glanced at the hand again, in envy. Nina went on slowly chewing. She was not so dazzlingly perfect as Amber, but prouder and fuller and easier to look upon, with a kind of inner strength in her hooded eyes and elegant thin nostrils.

"The youth revolution scene can't be aggression," Johnnie was saying, "can't possibly. Minds won't work in that groove anymore. It's like a child watching television . . ."

Child watching secret modest thighs against the table not two fingers away! And all unaware of me, or what I am!

The EAT man jumped in: "Obviously your generation is fed up with the old middle class platitudes."

"We're gonna make *new* middle class platitudes!" I jerked out like an adolescent. Nina went on munching but Tyrtan grinned directly with more understanding than I could bear.

Lollypop Rosenberg was staring coldly. Did he guess the jealousy, the desire?

"See something you like?" I inquired. This time it came out loud and clear, in the middle of no talk at all.

Rosenberg stood up, his lips in a tight line, and the photographer flashed his face. He turned his head away with a little smirk. "Time for household duties," he sniveled, and in a twinkling they'd all disappeared.

Had I been a boor? Unstylish maybe? Had Tyrtan had the nerve to rub my head in passing?

Outside I packed a snowball and let fly with all my might against a nearby tree. A patch of white plastered to the trunk as keen wet fragments whipped back in my face.

Stumping down the road I scooped snow from a stone wall and fired at a tree some twenty yards away. "Will I really make it, today, before the day is done?" I nicked my target, threw again on the same question and saw my snowball curve away as if turned by a magic hand.

"Marry Cathy?" I threw hard and careless, and produced a perfect hit. Threw again and missed by a mile.

"Do something worthwhile?" Missed. "Next year?" Missed. "Ever?" Nicked but so what? If only I could release it, let it all out, as beautifully as letting loose a snowball!

"Talent?"

"Genius?"

It was too ridiculous!

"Happy?" I charged through the woods throwing at one target after another, sending a flock of rooks up into the air cawing like a cootie-crop against the low grey sky.

On my seventh throw I hit a seedling no thicker than a lady's wrist while leaping in the air off a dead run sideways to the target. But I forgot what I was aiming for.

"Die?" Where did that question come from?

In the middle of the woods I came upon a long track where the snow was churned and stained a deep crimson. I could see where the deer had fallen from the impact of the bullet, struggled to her feet, and raced madly, sprinkling blood on trees and snow. She had fallen and got up again, running erratically, taking the blow of a second bullet, flailing and wobbling and coming to earth at last fifty yards uphill from the spot where the first shot had entered her body.

All that was left was a hollowed nest where the snow was packed with rich blood and the footprints of hunters. I knelt emptily in tribute, picked up some bloody snow and tasted it. A bloodsickle!

I plunged through deep snow, away from the footprints over a hill and into a little gully. I was beginning to be hollowed out from so many scenes, so many people coming on, but all the same I liked this mindless panicked plunging. Even the blank fear of it was better than my thought, much better and purer than any talk I knew. In my high school days in Kansas City I would take the car out at night and ride for miles across the plains, eighty to a hundred miles an hour, flat beat music blasting in my ears. Till at last my blessed brain was severed and I could go back home and crawl into bed.

Ploughing through the drifts I tripped and fell headlong and lay for a while covered. When I dug for what had felled me, I found a headstone from 1896 named Sarah Mayflower, and not far away, Joseph Mayflower 1890, with a little rhyme beginning "Now I lay me down to sleep. . . ." Crawling happily on hands and knees I exposed a dozen others dating back to the seventeenth century, including one titled "Lorna Coburn a witch" and a small flat stone with epitaph all in Hebrew.

Then it occurred to me there were people below lying chest to chest with me, shut forever in little boxes rotting away. I jumped up and scampered back to the road, followed it through deserted fields and orchards blanketed with snow. After an hour I had plodded past the last outbuilding and farmhouse where the snow was no longer flattened by the tracks of cars. Still I tramped on, refusing to return the way I'd come. By and by the road reached the edge of the estate, as I knew it must, and veered sharply to parallel the roadway on the other side of a high hedge.

I had come into an icy wind, and thrust my way leaning forward from the waist and piercing with my pointed head. Dismally I thought of my teachers and other men I knew in the world; shuffled them over in my mind, trying to think of one strong man or one happy man who was not an idiot. Yet all of them expected me to grow up somehow, to act, to choose. Why should I? What if I didn't? One foot, I put, and then the other.

The road at last completed its circuit and joined the entrance road not far from the stone gatehouse, so that I re-traveled the route I had driven the night before. Around me was the tunnel of evergreens, ahead the lake, the grove, the warm large house. I had walked too far; emerging from the evergreens I saw the sky shade to a sooty mauve fog that came close about me and clung palpably as I forced my way through. The thought of the long drive back to the city nagged at me. I wasn't ready, couldn't face people, lacked force even to operate the car.

I went out on the bridge and peered down to the frozen lake. The glassy surface sent up little shards of light, prismatic gleamings, flashes of green and yellow rainbow. Appealing to me. I could have rolled over the low bridgerail, my stomach relaxing at last in the soft dark, my body in a tremendous smack that would conclude everything.

I eased myself onto the rail and lay there, arms and legs dangling on either side, savoring my lack of fear.

As a child—no more than nine—I had stood one day bouncing a baseball against the boards of our white frame house. It was a game to see how many times I could cleanly field the carom. I built up to five, ten, thirteen. I could feel myself getting stronger and better every time. But a problem remained, always; I couldn't stand it; I offered up a mental prayer. "If I can't do it twenty times I'll kill myself, I mean it."

I did it twenty times. "Twenty-five!" I whispered. I threw hard and fielded cleanly five more times. "Fifty!" Fighting off my weariness my boredom I threw harder than ever and made inspired catches. Though I'd never been over nineteen I now miraculously had fifty. Fifty-one would be a magic number, a definite sign! ". . . and if I miss, I promise to take my life, no matter what!" A solemn bargain.

My mind boggled as I was about to let go. The ball squirted from my hand, bounced feebly against the boards, and plopped to earth. I dove, batted it loose, and lay watching helpless as it rolled seam over seam into a small puddle beneath the drainpipe. It quivered minutely, and the motion went out of it.

Heavy organ music from daytime serials. A kind of terrifying gladness. I went to my nest in a vacant lot.

"It didn't count," I said to God; "it slipped." But I knew that God said No. Finally I worked something out. "All right God," I said. "Remember I didn't say when. Maybe I'll be an old man. But I will do it."

I lay that night in a cold sweat, having lost my last chance to live forever. But now, stretched on the ice-cold bar, the memory did not disturb me in the slightest. The superstition had gone with everything else. I was able, if I chose, to flip over on my side and float down fifty feet with the greatest of pleasure. After all, I had promised. Keeping promises was as good a way as any.

Perhaps I would fall asleep. I sprawled increasingly inert, shapeless, unanimate, despite the hard bar pressing from chest to groin. An even chance, as my ankles untwined in sleep from the rail behind me, that I would fall to the left or right. I'd see then what fate had in store for me etc.

Yet I couldn't sleep. So I rolled off and hung by one hand. It was dangerous—my grip wasn't right. Besides that I heard voices coming. I had a nice thrilling time heaving back on the bridge. It was all a disgusting conceit!

Mayflower was coming, with Nina—or Noni. Thank God they hadn't seen! I dusted myself.

"Alex-babe!" piped Jacky. He was dressed in black patent boots, velour levis, a vinyl hunting coat and flat velvet cap in muted maroon. In the crook of his arm he carried a rifle with a suede-covered stock.

"Where'd you run off to?" he demanded. Nina merely nodded, bundled nicely in a navy peacoat. "I'm going back now," she said softly, and turned and walked off up the road. Before I could think I had thrown a snowball: but she did not turn as my missile swooped by her and smashed and skidded on the icy path. In an instant her cozy little figure had faded into the early darkness.

"What's this hunting bit?" I said to Jacky. "I thought your leader was against it?"

"Oh what the hey!" said Jacky. He raised his rifle and squeezed off a few imaginary rounds. "It's a matter of feeling your own presence. Law of nature: that's one thing I've learned. The species all feed off one another and we've got to protect each other too. All part of the same thing: killing, being killed, refrain from killing. If you can't accept it the pressure just dams up, and when the dam breaks you've got an impersonal mechanical abomination of a *war* on your hands baby! Upset the whole damn ecology and what's more you rationalize it!"

"Not me," I said meekly. "Not Dr. Tyrtan I guess either."

"No, he's not in that bag. But he won't judgmentalize either. He knows I kill. He just doesn't want to see it."

I bade adieu to Jacky and struggled up the road. My feet and hands were burning cold and head worn numb with buffeting. I longed only to get up inside that big warm house where lights were burning. I could make it I thought to the library, sink down in that cavernous chair near the fire, and dissolve myself in heat. Or there were books on the shelves with warm rich illustrations to play in upon my eyes and devour me: Russian Icons and Turkish Miniatures, Spanish Frescoes of the Romanesque Period, Persian Miniatures and Japanese Shrine Paintings, Early Buddhist Paintings from the Adjanta Caves of India, Greek and Israeli Mosaics from Byzantine Churches, Byzantine Frescoes from Yugoslav Churches, Egyptian Wall Paintings from Tombs and Temples and Mexican Wall Paintings from Aztecs and Mayans, Aboriginal Paintings from Aboriginals, Medieval Norse Stave Church Paintings, Czechoslovakian Miniatures from Romansque and Gothic Manuscripts, Ceylonese Buddhas from Underground Crypts, Consecrated Relic Tintings from Christian Catacombs, Irish Illuminated Manuscripts from pre-Georgian Druidical Sanctuaries. These would be mine; I needed them for matter—or just anything at all.

8

We ate dinner crouched on a rug in a septagonal parlor tucked off the main rooms of the first floor, where I wolfed bland stew and rice, swilled down with tea and cocacola. Not much taste to it—so I ate more. Tyrtan for his part carefully set aside his cubes of meat. As he ate his brown rice grain by grain, he talked in undertones to Nelson Rosenberg and Quentin. The few others ate silently: both Seymour and Nina were among the absent. Amber sat next to me and got me things but I had difficulty beginning to talk to her. I was too conscious of Tyrtan, very loose on his home grounds, watching me without trying, too cheaply amused by what he saw.

Before I knew it he was on his feet to leave—and suddenly he turned and knelt to murmur in my ear. He was merely saying stay another night. But he tickled me and made me scratch.

It occurred to me I was disappointed to find such ordinary folk who chattered aimlessly, mild and imitative even in religious business. Yet what right had I? As if they owed me anything! Tickle tickle!

My eating companions quickly dwindled down to Amber, Johnnie and Jacky Mayflower. With a happy pride that would have been most *gauche* in the rooms of Bunny from Kansas City, Mayflower fluttered in his coat pocket and produced a Prince Albert canful of marijuana.

"Smoke for joy?" he inquired.

"Imagine!" Amber said. "The minds of people who would take our grass away! I wonder-wonder what they're so afraid of!"

"Themselves," said Johnnie.

"Is that what it is?" Amber asked me. She draped her arm around my neck, lovely breasties softening my kidney. "Is that it, really?"

"Are you asking me, really?"

She threw her head back laughing, shaking loose that straight blond hair. "Piddle-pickle, that's what I say!" She laughed again in exactly the same way.

"What was that?"

Piddle-pickle: she told me so again. But her arm was cozy, and the least I could do was wrap my own around her, clumsily knocking her head but getting there eventually so that my hand rested on the sharp incurve of her hip. She squirmed in close and I kissed her hair fraternally. Jacky and Johnnie were busy discussing the mechanics of deep inhalation.

And so the four of us got vaguely high together. The pot wasn't strong; the salesman I guess had cut it with Lipton tea. But it was all the same to my three companions. Was that why I'd been left with them, safely excluded from whatever goings-on upstairs?

"Beautiful, beautiful," moaned Mayflower. "I'd like to have a happening at night in Central Park. With no one but beautiful people in beautiful costumes and beautiful lights in trees and at the bottom of the reservoir."

"Since we're all so beautiful," I said, "we can meet in the daytime with no clothes on."

Amber said "Yes, let's! With flowers!"

"With worms," I said.

"With maggots," said Johnnie.

I fell back nuzzling Amber's clavicle: the scent of her, the bodyheat, the slide of her jersey. But she disengaged and rummaged in a floppy bag, producing a pair of rose-orange shades which had to be fit on carefully with both hands, leaving only sharp young elbows for me to clutch at. I lay back patiently and took a deep drag on the weed.

"If my old man could see us he'd pass gas," said Johnnie with a happy American grin that wrinkled his nose so cute.

"His father is not to be believed!" cooed Amber.

"He's a highschool principal," Johnnie explained to me. "All day long he deals with forms and slips and cards. When some actual kid is brought in you can see him to begin to crumble. If it's a spade he just boots 'em out, but with your ordinary white-middle j.d. he gives his little lecture on 'the spirit of service in the Peace Corps.' His head is clogged with rubbish of used-up symbols. Kids walk the halls out of their minds on A and he doesn't know it, doesn't even see them. As long as they pass their tests he's in the clear. Communication is like completely out of the question. He communicates with the women's clubs, rings these little bells like 'doctor' and 'lawyer' and they chirp 'That's my sonny!' "

Johnnie sucked hard on a roach, his soft face twisted with bitterness.

"It's okay though," I said. "I mean now you know, so what harm can he do you?"

He looked at me with contempt. I thought of my own scene back at the hotel.

"Okay, okay," I said, and Johnnie broke out immediately with his big open comradely smile.

"Are you serious?" he said. "Here's a man who has kids literally dying, starving, all around him and he gets a citation from some national foundation to preserve the fucking suburban American home! So we have 'marital hygiene' and movies of so-called 'pot addicts' and imbecile psychologists roaming the washrooms! Free therapy at the breakfast table, pray together stay together—in the inside of a plastic refrigerator! Bad news, man, he couldn't even hold *my Mother!* She had to clear out five years ago. She was going up the walls with boredom. His idea of a good marriage scene was to take her to 'functions' where she had to stand holding up her little teacup or cocktail and simper out his ugly little lies. Now they all say 'tsk, tsk, the poor boy has an alcoholic mommy.' But I'll tell you something man: I love that woman dearly. Whatever she may be she came to it because deep down she has soul. No matter how dead they drag her, she lives!"

Johnnie jumped up and spun around twice, making finger-crosses on his chest and forehead. "Whop whop whop!" he shouted, then plopped down with his angel grin to me.

"Don't mean to bug you man. Pardon my one bad track."

"I'm really into something with these lenses," said Amber. She was staring at a candle. She looped the sunglasses around my ears and helped me look by laying her cheek along mine, all sweetly unthinking.

"Let's drop all the way down!" said Johnnie. He began fiddling with knobs and buttons on a control board behind the player piano.

"We call it 'the machinator,' " said Amber in tiny-voiced elegance.

Sounds of music began to grind out slowly, as if from the bottom of a well. Then a stab of lightning shot the lights out. Thither and yon a flash of incandescent color as guitars flung whining spasms—and I saw the shadow of a man rise up with long knob counter of tape recorders, soundbooms, earphones, to take it all in. Wire string notes fell now like sonic booms and hot light flickers probed and cut with electric intensity. Amber and Johnnie were dancing together without touching, feet dangling and arms in a sinuous wobbling, bodies curling, coiling, spines slack chins loose eyes shut tight in agony as beams from tiny wall apertures painted them with strips of ancient movie.

Sweet Amber, mouth a flowerbud of infant corruption, bumped her childsmall hips and thrust her precious rosy groin in torment of ecstasy. Johnnie too rolled and thrust identically slim knees and thighs and waistline, identical boysmooth buttocks, face clenched exquisitely for yielding utter yielding as the limbs of him melted in jelly of napalm light.

The twanging twingtwonged louder, fiercer, swelling the room at its seams, shredding soundwaves into fine electric shrapnel to prick the pores of the skin and penetrate anus and ureter in a twitching itching slither, penetrate the lips the nostrils the corners of the eyes, flood the inner ear and shoot screwdrivers to the brainstem.

Voices shouting cockney fake hillbilly nasals chanting can't-don't-won't to a rhythm of can-do-will went pounding on unhearable up and down their chordbeads like a covey of baby tanks, rolling on through whatever country, laying flat all opposition.

Jacky Mayflower lay on his back wriggling in violet light, voluptuous if chubby, squirming sighing as he wrenched off his vest. Oh he quivered, massaging his stomach, face mirroring a rapture of violation from our blossoms twining in the middle writhing open and shut their petals in glorious offer of rape. Optical paintings dithered in opalescent panelings, slid Indian dancers in coldfire as bands of light revolved across them, each giving way to another from inside him, inside her, weaving snakesupple arms beneath headdress of perpetual hands and eyes.

And what of myself then, waiting on the shingle, should I turn not pale belovèd snail? I flew up into the middle of it stretching out like rubber reaching pulling flexing shaking it all down loose. The other two bathed face to face but I was off in my sphere, all separate, enclosed, enveloped in the static tonewail, moving respectfully, unsorting it, putting it out and leaving it, reaching back for it and letting it go, showing at last the free live moments of the longheld one, the one of grace and power streaming out now with power's lovely energy brought up from too long hampered red bloodcells of being, incredible lovegift belonging to me only, the one, the center, the real, alone at last complete and imperturbable, wonder of all, warm and free in the center of the only, the one and only, again and forever now coming true.

We swam through an ocean of sound in long exotic armpulls, our bodies greased with excretions of soulstuff sealing us warm and fluid. Here and there foaming tapenoises burst to the surface: sea-sounds, long groans, bellows and creakings. And the rush of an express-train, the drawn-out fingernail of metal brakes on naked rails, the ringling of its little bell and the hiss of steam from the boiler. A jet plane roared on through, shaking the walls of the skull, while all the little bones rattled with the fire of jungle machineguns. A politician spoke stirringly of our way of life boys fighting to defend and their mothers drowned out in the fall of a six-car collision brake drums pounding off and on like battering of tides torn loose from the moon. The floor itself revolved and turned us slowly baking in the crossfire of light as we writhed and rambled slipping easily the beams of fire while the turntable raised us on high and sank us down again deeper than before.

The piercing needle lights relaxed and fell out blobs of haze: a heavy fog came on, rich garbage smell, and I could barely see the double image of my dear ones jerking now like twitched rope-ends among the empty cups and plates of supper. Their limbs hopped torsoes collapsing heads sapped tossing like poppies in a dark breeze the nerve-circuits jammed and firing away to the last gone end. I sank to my knees, an odor of violets enveloping me, too thick, too pungent for a single set of nostrils to comprehend. My nose ears eyes all other openings completely plugged with atmospheric lunch. And even the others were grinding down soon. . . .

In the next world the music slowed and died, the usual lights came on, the two young beauties flopped their arms about each other's necks as the flux of sensory fog receded. On the far shore I glimpsed the recording man fold his apparatus neatly into the wall and depart without a glance gripping in each fist an attaché case. The couple now: I scrutinized them. Would there be contact, had they screwed themselves to the sticking point? Not so, not even relevant: they clung like tired pups, separate as mirror images, plastic and alive back then now soft and wilted in a played-out glory. They fell apart like halves of a poisoned flower.

"So many ways!" gasped Johnnie.

"And zap!" said Jacky—"There's no guilt!"

The four of us lay flopped on the rug, Amber with her head in my lap. "The only time I'm whole," she murmured, and let herself limp in sexless exhaustion.

"Like an electric shock," said Johnnie ten minutes later, "that rewires your whole system."

"But I feel the same," I said sadly.

"You weren't really in there," Mayflower diagnosed.

Whether or not I was still alas too much whatever I was. Too aware of the girl stretched out before me, the open fact of her, the inner and outer parts. Surprisingly she stirred, as if I stirred her. She was reviving, she wanted to show me something—took my hand and pulled me from the room.

But Johnnie came running down the hall and caught us. Clutching our hands in his he looked with pale tired joy from one to the other. Jumping on tiptoe he leaped into my free arm, resting his elbows on my shoulder and whispering through fine cupped hands: "I'm so glad you're here, Alex! Enjoy yourself: Do!" Whereupon he whirled away, pirouetted, and vanished in the twinkling of a pupil.

I followed her through intricate passageways to the back of the house, I think, where we entered a small room plated with mirrors on all six inner surfaces. Sweetly she gestured and I lay as bidden on one of the mats which were the room's only furnishings, watching her as sylph-like she glided lighting candles and incense-sticks, dropping at last in a rush of lovely flesh beside me on her stomach. She had a book; she wanted to read to me. The small cones of her breasts touched perfect to the mat inside the points of her propped elbows.

In a wall-mirror I watched her soft child lips as she read dwellingly from a book of Zen wisdom. Ah sagedom profound simplicity etc irrelevant to the pink insides of the corners of her mouth or to my predicament as I sprawled on my side, on my back, twisting insatiable for more than meaning. I looked up to the ceiling mirror, where I saw, through the flickering light, her skirt lifted, long straight legs in black tights, delicious hollows of the backs of her knees, and above them the lower parts of her thighs. I could imagine the feel of elastic in my hands, the snugness each morning as she pulled the cloth close to the gentle parts beneath her skirt. The backs of my own thighs tingled in apprehension of touching hers. "Here it is," I heard once more—a whisper in my inner ear of mad perfection still to be enjoyed. It did exist, it must, for those who could reach out, who had it in them to dare, truly, from a core of destined deserving.

If you reached out doubting, reached not high enough, lacking that inner core, what could happen, finally, but mere hints and flashes and half-baked memories? What were you at bottom but a coward masturbator?

She shifted to one elbow, stretching each fine long fiber. Her modeled face turned to mine pouting, wide-eyed, sensual-dreamy. "You see," she said, "ever since it all began, all the wise men have been saying the same thing . . . but no one listens."

I groaned with weight of desire. "No one listens to me either!"

She rocked equisitely in my direction, moving closer, then fixed for an instant in balance. She looked up from within kissing distance, vague turquoise eyes all earnest, uneven, swimming madly to get me in focus. I leaned very near, nearer than she knew.

"What do you think of Spengler?" she asked.

My wicked reflex had me laughing, though I knew so well it would never do. She was merely baffled, rolled over on her back away from me, slowly bringing down her lids like white silk windowshades on her lovely wide blurred eyes.

"Spengler's all right," I said, moving my palm so lightly across the grain of hers.

"I saw him last night," she said quickly.

"Oh?"

I leaned over her as she lay with eyes shut, surveying

her in a kind of luxury, pot-calm, languid, pleasantly tired. Her eyes flew open, shot past me straight to their own reflection in the ceiling. She began to talk rapidly.

"We discussed the spiral. History spirals. Light is bent, you know. It spins round and round and out the other end. Like the human body, the soma. I know you've taken courses in cell biology. Spengler told me, he knew perfectly well eons and epochs ago. It's all the same, the particles of the body spin in a perfect spiral. That's why death can never really happen."

Shaken, I put my hand to her cheek. But she was coming along five minutes behind me: she flung her arms about my neck and drew me down, kissing me and squirming sleekly, preciously the whole length of her to her toes. Pressing so tight I could not move she went on talking, strewing her words in helpless anguish. I could feel through my cheek the tiniest tongue movements as she went on talking.

"Now, now, I can feel it coming! I was having a child you see. A reincarnation. And the child was spiralling inside me. I imagined a terrible hurting, because I was taught as a baby my pain was real. I was terribly sick, my head was sick. I was fighting to push it away, I didn't want it, I didn't want to live. It hurt to breathe; I held my breath until I choked. . . ."

She thrust me away, staring as if she had never seen me before.

"It's all right," I said stupidly. "Your friend Alex." But was I her friend? I stroked her arm, so long and fragile. She didn't acknowledge: it was all so far away. Just a little arm-stroke, miss—see my hand out there?

"You know what I mean?" she said intently. "Have you ever had the Drug?" I shook my head. "Well, you'll see. You'll use your head. Everyone does. It helps you get well. That's why I came here, so many moons ago, so many rivers running under a bridge. Do you know the riddle of the rivers? It's one of the oldest riddles there is. I was a tiny dollbaby without a head and without any clothes on. I had plastic skin and arms and legs that swiveled all the way around. And in between my legs it was smooth, you see—that's what made the pain! But my karma took me here, to the now, and I got all born again, ever so gently. I grew inside a tulip like a little elf, and I stretched myself, and I blossomed out, and I was radiant. . . ."

She lay stiffly with an arm beneath her neck, staring up again at her image in the ceiling. I watched cautiously, having captured a portion of her sleeve. She sat up with a sparkling smile and took my hand.

"Have you ever taken anything else?"

"Some things," I said.

"They put a needle in my arm," she said dreamily. "They were the kindest people. All the modern poets were there, the ones that count. They wanted only to help me, to guide me on my path. And so they gathered round and put it into me, and after my child was born they brought me here. . . ."

She trailed off. "What happened to the child?" I asked.

Amber jumped to her feet in yet one more uncoiling of energy. She lit fresh incense sticks, blew out half the candles, tore open a glassine envelope and shook phosphorescent powder into the air.

"This is our exercise room," she announced. "Do you know the Disciplines?"

"Only in a general way," I said.

She knelt on the mat and tucking her head to her knees rolled forward on her neck thrusting her short-skirted bottom into the air. She rocked, and rocked, and sat back dazed. "Oh Wow!" she said.

She made me kneel and put me through the same business, boldly handling my haunches. As I too rolled on my neck I heard her say, "There's so many paths to ecstasy. . . . You should do this all the time. No, no, you've got to roll, really stretch your neck."

She put her hand between my legs and rocked me forward hard.

"Your body releases NT-390. That's it! Now sit up."

Two waves rippled dizzily from the sides, collided and bounced back again. The room shimmered, blurred, flickered in the flame of a candle. I shook my head, my vision popped together. I saw myself reflected in the wall before me, a seated Buddha reduplicated to infinity, the blonde girl forever by my side.

Having dominated, she knelt more confidently, but I was all too aware and flung myself like a savage, pinning her down, kissing her mouth and stroking her.Yet dammit —I released her. Because really she didn't want to. She caught her breath, propped on one hand. I would not look at the reflections: or the captive creature who sat lumpishly burning at their crossing-point.

Still the girl reached softly to my forearm with a tentative actual smile. She was beckoning again, God knew why. I had been given one more cycle. I might proceed to the end now, possess what had been promised, even blindly, without knowing or caring if it came to that, so long as I did not lose or fail or miss out. And there I was in the mirror, cackling at me like a monkey!

Down, monkey! I would take it proper and slow this time. With gentle big fingers I gently stroked her hair. The stars in her eyes dissolved to a tender slowness. For a moment I saw her as a woman, in all her potential. But she fell in a heap, undone. Curled up on her side in a hard little knot.

Sorry at last, stupefied, shocked out of my cock, I had sense to back off and let her get to the door.

Doorknob in hand, she struck one last pose.

"I think I'm going to fast for a few days," she said.

"Me too," I mumbled, to a closed door.

Five minutes later I was knocking at Dr. Tyrtan's room. After a long silence the door opened and Quentin came out, powering around me with the grace of a middleweight. "Alex?" called a voice from within. Tyrtan lay on a velvet couch reading a book I knew on supergalactic clusters. Letters notebooks and ledgers lay scrambled on the floor.

"Just a little something," I said.

"Of what?" Tyrtan swung up into an intense concentration.

"About the girl."

A corner of his mouth turned up, an eyebrow arched —"Well?"

"I'm uh concerned," I said. About what? I couldn't think.

"And so is she concerned about you."

Tyrtan was giving me the full grin now.

"I'm so glad you two have found each other," he said.

"She can't find anybody," I blurted. "She's sick."

Tyrtan sighed, shook out a cigarette from a nearby jar. "Most interesting," he said. "That's quite a concept."

"No concept," I said. "She's not with it, she doesn't know what's going on."

"And where are you?" he said.

"I don't get it."

He yawned and stretched full length with hands locked under his flaming neck-curls. "What gives you the right," he said to the ceiling, "to define the electric impulses that pass through your own head as healthy, and hers as sick?"

"Who is defining?" I said.

"That's just it!" He laughed softly. "I heard something about you, Alex . . ."

He paused; I could hear my heart bump faster.

"I heard you took a bet once to talk all night about Plato—and you won, didn't you?"

It was only that. I was pleased.

"Tell me something," he continued. "Exactly what did you talk about?"

"Hell, I don't know. Lots of things. I babbled away."

"The one and the many?" he asked.

"Mostly the many."

"But what is the one?" he asked slowly.

God's asshole, I almost said. Not this again! "I'll tell you later," I said.

"Then don't you know?"

"Do you?"

"I'll tell you later."

He laughed again in his lazy way. "You're really a good person Alex. No doubt about it. I get the most amazing vibrations. You want to help people. The idea of insanity disturbs you. You look at your roommate, you look at Amber—and you want them to operate in terms of reality. But as you just admitted, you don't even know what reality is—"

Suddenly he swooped out on velvet ropes of laughter. "I can't help it," he gasped. He lay weakly, clutching his belly. "You must think I'm very rude, forgive me, please, it's not you, not at all. . . .

"It's just that we've up-leveled all that. If you only knew. . . . But you will know! It isn't necessary anymore. The surface game level means very little. . . ."

"But she's in pain!" I said. "She's scared, she's all screwed up inside!"

"Forgive me, Alex." He sat up again, leaned his forearms on his knees, and pondered the strip of carpet between his feet. He was deliberating very hard it seemed—not a trace of humor in his face now.

I waited. "Of course," he said finally, "one can see the fear in a given person. But what it means, and what one has the right to do about it, are different questions. Sometimes it's best to *accept* the fear, if you know what I mean?"

"Yes, yes," I said. "But what if someone's still on the verge of panic, always, no matter what?"

The man got up, startling me, and stretched and slapped me on the shoulder.

"Frankly I question your whole concept of insanity, Alex. That's not what it's all about. And you're so close to seeing that! Excuse me, I'm laughing again—"

He leaned against the frame of a casement window, the pane of which was set with tiny circles of stained glass. Wheezing he struggled to control his laughter, all the time bobbing his head as if to faint jazz from the speakers in the wood outside.

I stepped toward him, thinking what fun to push my fist in his soft laughing mouth.

But Tyrtan threw up his arms and staggered backwards, shaking his head. "I don't blame you!" he cried. "To you I'm psychotic, yes I know, believe me, I know that!"

He stopped me cold. I saw he was laughing at more than myself, laughing at everything, openly, the whole bit.

He managed then to master his face; only the brilliant eyes betrayed the glee thrust down within. And I saw the glee was partly for me—to have me there. "It's all right," he said. "Don't say a word. Stop." It was all right, mostly. We stood calmly looking at one another. "You're right," he said, "Amber's insane, and I am myself perhaps truly psychotic. I'm not arguing, honest: not with you. You're too beautiful, Alex, you play the game better than they ever want anyone to play it—so well you're going to blow it apart!"

I was laughing—I couldn't help it. The man was too much. He sprang close and caught my elbows in his hands.

"Let me tell you a secret."

He searched my eyes as I stood twitching, giddy, frowning, laughing.

"One level of reality is as good as any other," he said.

Jacky was right: I was never really in there.

I ran away, straight up to my room, where I sat among the tapestries like a boy scout in his tent.

At last I pulled my ponderous shoes off. The mattress had been freshly ensheeted: throwing back the figured bedspread I discovered a new-cut book wrapped in slick oilskin and covered in buckram stamped with fiery wheels and many-armed dancers. Stripped down to my underwear I snuggled in and began to read by candlelight. Books at least were copeable.

The book was a manual, it said, by Magus Tyrtan M.D. and Nelson Rosenberg M.S., detailing the spiritual preparation for a "journey" with the Answer Drug. The main idea was to rewrite an ancient Mongolian scripture on death and rebirth in terms of what the "traveler" could expect from the Drug. But I never can focus when people start in lumping. Here were scraps of medicine and physics mixed in with Bardos, Tantrics, Vedics, visions and divinites. To say nothing of world politics: "The present moment in human history—as Lama Kuzi Yawa-

Gumpinda points out—is critical." Newsflash from the Lamastery! My eye caught a footnote distinguishing between the fundamental Wisdom Teachings, the Divine Body of Truth, the supra-mundane All-Consciousness, the Holy Body of Perfect Endowment, the Essential Wisdom, the Incarnate Wisdom, the Threefold Principle of the Cause of all Causes, the All-Pervading Essence of Spirit, and the Exoteric Trinity of Buddha Scriptures and Priesthood.

Metaphor or what? I tried to read more seriously. The "Bardos," I learned, were a series of conscious states through which the traveler might pass, half of them ecstatic and half-nightmarish, with appropriate hallucinations for each. If you knew where you were going, you could latch on to the ecstasy and purge the horror. The book ended in a chain of incantations to ease the traveler up the trail to the ultimate transcendence.

It had to be serious, yes? The book was put together with loving care and moreover a precision, a sureness referable to some definite external standard which I failed to grasp. Because of ultimate Druglessness? Fighting off sleep I went back to the beginning. It seemed the first vision was the best, so overwhelming in fact that the average psyche simply refused to let it happen. While novices and those beset by "ego-defenses" slipped straight into lesser Bardos, the truly open voyager could shed the bonds of ego and attain a glimpse of the Clear Light. This moment was the crown in the treasure of racial knowledge locked somehow into every cell of the body and releasable by the neurological timekey, whatever that was, of the Drug. . . .

But I failed again, I lost track: my eye went on reading while my mind had vacated. So I flipped over on my stomach, insides protected from an easy stabbing, and fell asleep before the candle gutted.

A cracking woke me half a night later. I lay in the dark listening to faint scrapes and snatches of voice and slowly explained to me where I was. Meanwhile I held fast my boyish tassel to fend off sudden inevitable dread. Someday soon I would not be. But the trick was not to think, to drift back to sleep with sweet power of sex-dreams. What did old men do, I feared, when body softened and best chances lay behind? The whole trick in flipping off lay in believing the images—that somehow somewhere someway they must come true. The pit gaped for me—I must not grow old! Get out of it somehow. No more think.

In a while the Nazis would come and force us into flesh-packed barrels. Sorry, Ma'am, nothing I can do! But it wasn't quite . . . it kept slipping. . . .

Because of him? He'd been watching for some time. *The little man,* his hat pulled low over huge ugly head! From the shadow where his eyes lurked he had seen it all. He waited now, for me, as he'd waited through years of nightmares, waited with implacable will to kill my Daddy!

Whether from sleep or waking I jumped up weeping screaming and threw the heavy vellum book into the corner with all my might.

9

A STREAM OF SUNLIGHT shot through the little porthole to irradiate my cheek. Opened my eyes—and there was Dr. Tyrtan, bending fondly over, grinning that completely open boyish grin. Damned if he didn't chant something, maybe tinkle a few finger cymbals.

"You're growing, Alex. You're an opening bud. I dig what you've been going through here, even the suspicion. But your eyes are open, right? You've got to look! Cigarette?"

"Don't know . . ." I groaned. I wanted to urinate—to say nothing of my morning erection. Did Tyrtan observe? So what? Yet I was not about to hop up at a disadvantage. Meanwhile the man's lips were moving: ". . . simply that you're still seeking. You haven't latched on to anybody's status quo."

"Including yours."

"Mine?" He mimed puzzlement. "Oh yes. The master pusher—won't be satisfied till every teeny schoolchild mainlines noon and night. I'm with you, I'm way out in front. But you know that's not really why the authorities wig out at the very mention of my name."

"Um-hmn." My erection had gone down some. I got out gingerly and slipped on my pants. Then I had to sit down, because Tyrtan was standing right in front of me and the room was too small.

"They panic," he said, "because they see it crumbling, the whole verbal edifice of Western history. It's going to come smashing down soon, Alex, no matter what happens to creatures like you and me."

"Then cancel my reservation," I yawned.

Tyrtan stood staring down at me, chin cupped in crotch of thumb and forefinger.

"You think you don't have the slightest idea of what I'm talking about."

Since he was not about to move, I flipped my legs back in bed and pulled the covers up to my chin.

"You had nightmares," he announced.

"What makes you think so?"

"You forget I've spent a good part of my life in hospitals. I recognize that haunted look. If it weren't for the dazzling energy that shines from your eyes, why . . . I'd think you were a badly hung-up person, Alex."

"You talk like a shrink!"

He covered his head. "Heaven forbid."

"Well aren't you? Sort of free-lance?"

He bowed. "Merely your local ex-medical doctor. Face-to-face only, low downpayment, no terms. I was in deep psychoanalysis for years," he went on brightly, "but I didn't get anywhere. I had terrible resistances."

The glee was back in his face. It maddened me.

"You talk as though it's a joke—as though everything you say is a joke!"

"You mean it's *not* a joke?"

It was fun to hear him say so, but still . . .

"Well what makes hangups like yours or mine?"

He wasn't stuck for an answer. "Take a baby three–four–five days old, lying in his crib. Now that baby is *completely high*; every second, billions of impulses bombard his eye at the speed of light—and so far he has no filtering mechanism, he's in raptures! Then at one point a face comes down and says, "Ooh, aren't you a bad boy, you're all wet!"—and bang! there was that face, or maybe it was the bars of the crib. Whatever your accident of imprinting was, that was it, and ever since you've spent an increasing amount of lifetime developing a reward-punishment good-bad system to justify that original imprint."

Tyrtan was peering out the tiny window, biting his nails as he talked, his eyes lit up and shining as the words poured through his fingers.

"What about me?" I prompted. "Is it too late?"

"All depends," he smiled. "But you'll have to kick that dialectic habit. Plato had a great soul, but his method was pure defense. We've got to move to an entirely new level of discourse—or maybe it's not new; it began really with Einstein, but biology never caught up. To say nothing of politics. And your average educated man has the mental habits of a Newton. But there are young ones growing who aren't hooked, they haven't *learned* what you and I have, Alex. They've learned to travel in inner space—as natural for them as breathing. They're the ones who will finish the whole up-leveling of medicine. What a kick it must be to sit in their suburban high schools and junior highs, looking down on their teachers from a million light-years above and beyond!"

"But what about you?"

"Oh well," he said, "there's always trepanning. I've had a tiny hole drilled in my skull which lets in just enough oxygen for steady flight."

We shared an inside laugh.

"And then you always have the Drug," I reminded him.

"You'll have it too," he said. "If not now, then later, when the tide breaks, and you'll need some sort of craft to float with the current. You won't want to drown! And all around you you'll see skimming the new thinkers, new scientists, new artists. . . ."

He fell off into a reverie. "Artists too?" I prodded.

"Yes! Because we've up-leveled the arts as well, almost by accident! There won't be novels anymore or weighty tragedies and so forth—art will invoke free combinations, chance movements, the serene randomness of play. Of course there is no such thing as chance or accident. Only radiant complete concurrences! *Angst* is dead, my friend; beginning now, the supreme artists are those and only those who know how to join in the cold clear cosmic laughter."

"And the price of admission?" I asked by rote.

"The obliteration of self. Oddly enough, it's exactly the program of Mao, a poet and visionary much misunderstood in the Western world. Notice how he's dismantling cities, bugging the bureaucracy, setting loose swarms of free youth: he wants a return to the tribal order, where there's no social obstruction between the consciousness and the cosmos."

"Lumping and more lumping!" I exclamed, all twitchy from lying still holding my piss and having to listen.

"Yes, maybe—for people like you."

"People like me! How the hell do you know what I am or who I'm like?"

"Look! Look!" squealed Tyrtan. He grabbed up the manual where it lay on its spine in the corner, and tore out a blank binding page. Produced a black crayon and with elegant fingers, blood ring flashing, he drew a thick circle.

"Now here's you. This circle is filled with pessimism, stoicism. You hate it, but you think you have to put up with it." He marked off a small sector. "But this little part, deep down in your brain, is straining with hope. You know what it's hoping for? Ecstasy! That's why we've met!"

Before I could question he drew another circle and stabbed it wildly as he struggled for words. "Now here's me! Here's me! In my case"—he drew a circle inside his circle, swelling against it—"my whole area is filling up to the point where I'll be all hope, all ecstasy!"

"Why then . . . you're pregnant!"

"Oh no!" Tyrtan rose from his knees, stretched his arms to the ceiling, laughing softly, almost blissfully. "I'm just beginning. I told you that. I'm not a spiritual leader. Not yet."

I myself felt gritty and disembodied, lying covered with only my head in action and mouth full of foul sleep and decay.

"Gee whiz Dad, can I be a spiritual leader too? I mean, what can a person do, once he's gone and learned something?"

He gave me his evilest grin, the divine put-on, as if he knew, deep down, how desperately I really meant it.

"No need to do. No need to strive. As the sages tell, lean, lean towards it, and ye shall fall into it. The Void—"

He was interrupted by a piercing scream, whereupon he shut his mouth and walked smoothly from the room. I followed in a dash for the water closet. By the time I re-emerged there was nothing to be seen but empty corridor.

Around the bend I came upon a little woman in a baggy kimono, standing on tiptoes to peek into a gilt-cherubed wall-mirror. "Would you kindly please sir lift me up?" She had the voice of a nymphet ten-year-old.

I held her up, all ninety pounds of her, while she

stabbed deftly at her elfin face, blackening the rims of her huge black eyes and filling fibrous material into the creases of her mouth. "My name is Mona Sweetan," she piped sexily. "I'm what's called a lady poet. You can find my books in the Library of Congress, but don't bother unless you care to sit down and read with all your heart. I don't write for people who fancy themselves poetic."

She fluffed down the pixie darts of her grey-streaked hair.

"Well you're a nice young hunk," she said. "Have you ever slept with a woman?"

"Have you ever taken the Answer Drug?" I countered.

"Just once"—dusting final powder on the ends of her lashes. "I must admit my generation had hard times with cream and drug-berries. We prefer liquor and sex. But you young ones have to have your medicine. My own son is zonked out half his waking life. Probably began with all those vitamins I crammed down his gullet.

"But don't let me hurt your feelings. I wanted badly to try the damn thing, but once it started happening I resisted. Being a game little chippie I fought it all the way. So I got frightened. Never so frightened of anything. But never fear—I'll try again. I hear you get beyond that. I think I know my own hangups, after all this time. You think it would happen again? Or what?"

Her fingers fiddled with her tubes and vials while her black sharp pupils sought my face in the mirror. Suddenly the eyes blurred, the little mouth began to tug, a streak of color ran. I set her down.

"You'll be all right," I said.

"It's funny," she said rapidly, unabashedly sniffling; "that happens sometimes when I remember. The only way to stop it cold is to try again. It's like jumping back in the water after you've nearly drowned. I used to be quite a thing for swimming. I suppose they only want my money but I like them very much. To me they're the only ones who are fresh and new."

She was too fast for me. "That doesn't mean," I deliberated, "that you should—"

"I cast sticks this morning," she said. She put her hand inside my belt and hung there, yearning up at me with overwhelming hopefulness. "I have a prime number. I've had visions all my life. I don't have to take anything. Once I went wild on nothing but nutmeg. I remembered things from another life. I foretold the future. I knew I'd be in this house this very day."

She nuzzled her soft-cut little head in my belly. I felt fingers creeping in my fly and stepped carefully back. Miss Sweetan cocked her sharp face up, deep eyes full of pain. "All right," she said. "The old woman will leave you alone. Thanks for the lift."

She winked and swung off down the corridor, her kimono flapping like a couple of signboards. The best I could do was stand and watch like a lecher—and be rewarded with a dashing shimmy as she spun from sight.

I heard a panicky giggling and slipped down a flight of stairs in mild foreboding. Seymour was stalking my old friend Amber, and she backing off like a nervous animal. Seymour had come into motion: his shirt was off, revealing a flaccid hairless front which hung out over his tight-checked pants. I could see his small eyes glitter behind those lenses as he came on step by step, jerking back his flaxen hair. Amber was giggling, gasping, licking her lips, pursing them now in a delectable pout. At last she broke the spell with a tiny shriek and ran mincingly away. Seymour bounded after her and lay his white hand on her arm. She screamed silently and slid off around a corner.

Amber pattered up a carved stairwell and came to a stop, confused, in dead center of the house where stairs and windows stretched away at careening angles. But Seymour had stepped out on the roof—he jumped in heavily through a balcony window. Amber ran into an adjacent garret. I heard her gasp: the room was covered with spiders, dangling from every cranny—red plastic spiders, fuzzed and furry spiders, real spiders suspended in jars, hopping up and down in their excitement. Spiders on the bedspread, the walls, spinning webs on the windows; green spiders underfoot, hooktoothed spiders on the pillow, hairy spiders scurrying beneath the sheets.

I heard her shriek with laughter as Seymour drew near. "Is this your room?" she cried, "You're really into something!"

I was standing on the top rung of the staircase, looking through the open door at an angle, wanting to move, to do . . . what? With what right? But in a moment he would—a tap on my shoulder! I spun round, nearly losing my footing, to find the hulking Quentin deadpan up against me. Even from the next lower step, he loomed taller. I could see the hair in his nostrils, smell the sweet effulgence of his armpits.

"Can I help you?" he intoned.

"Not that I know of."

"We mind our own business here," he said wittily.

"Good policy," I agreed.

A tension developed. Considering my leverage and quickness, I might perform an experiment in old-fashioned Newtonian shoving. But behind me the desperate giggles subsided into silence. Then a moan of some sort.

What the hell, I stepped around him, carefully, and went down.

Mona Sweetan was waiting for me. "I saw it all. He's a vulgar bully."

"What bugs me," I said, "is what he thought he was stopping me from."

"Don't let it bother you. You know what I mean. Look at me, Alex. I really mean this."

Too much, much too much! "I have to get clothed," I said, nodding at my undershirt. I finished dressing in the bathroom, where jagged stripes transect the ceiling and mirrors sparkle with holy stenciled syllable of "OM."

Downstairs I phoned and again no answer. Made sense: if yesterday he's asleep, today he's bound to be out. Cathy might know; but her phone was busy—and busy, apparently off the hook.

I went outdoors and wandered in back near a big stone empty basin with an Indian statue in the middle. Water supposed to spout from elephant's trunk. Sign on nearby tree: press button for magic fountain happening. Pressed button: nothing happening. Efflatus Elephantiasis? Sound of faroff peanut shells? Nothing.

I sat brooding in the basin. A spade gardener came by, saw me, and went the other way.

It was a day of sun and bright cloud, and the shadows of the clouds came racing across the hills. Sitting precisely I let myself be swept with sun and shadow. My mind turns over, like a heavy bale, from one frustration to another. I feel somehow I'm thirteen again and the old man takes us out after supper to divide up the yard work. Somehow I won't agree—on principle, no doubt. Billy would say nothing, do whatever he pleased. But it seems after fifteen minutes I won't see reason, proposing by then it's ridiculous to cut trim etc, let it grow wild why not, put in wild fruit, animals: I propose a vote. Power politics in play, only old Dad out of his head. Suspense broke at last he clubs stomps uses hoe handle. Me/him: us/them. Billy wanders off to movies while I sulk under boards in a vacant lot, rubbing my bones with mulch, choking in moral outrage.

I creep at last from my hideout and run like crazy, on and on into the mild dark, far out beyond the suburbs across the vale of highways and deep in muddy fields.

No moon out, but a sky clotted with furry stars. I could see like a cat, I said, and had no trouble moving through the fields and up the low thin-wooded hills. A night breeze cooled my bruised skin; I breathed deep, as I walked, of the cooling air. My eyes were bathed and clear from crying, and I could almost laugh with each last coughing sob. I knew I could run again if I had to, or suffer a razor strop or any other blow that would come my way. My body knew a kind of exaltation. I was going to get stronger as I went along, and I thought that meant I must prevail.

I walked for hours. That was the night I saw two men fighting behind a drive-in. Or was it another night? They had pounded in sullen fury for more than an hour, till their muscles were so beaten they could hardly lift their arms. In the crisscross of headlights they lurched together, heaving in ponderous underwater lunge-outs; slipping in the mud, bracing, grappling not to fall. The crowd of young men laughed and cursed, hopped out of the way and surged back in again.

Finally one got a club and the other a brick; brick stepped through club and landed a blow to the head. The other staggered back, straight at me. I was grabbed and thrown where the weight of the retreating crowd pressed me up against the stucco wall of the drive-in. I twisted to get loose, tore my shirt and chafed my back on the rough wall. Just in time to see the down man slip his picket between the legs of his oncoming enemy. The other boy went down and was kicked in the neck, writhed almost free and got kicked again in the gut. While he lay on his back gasping for breath the top man planted his foot on his wrist and broke his arm with one careful crack-of the club.

The boy with his arm broke let out a cry of animal pain. He got to his feet somehow, free hand still clutched to his brick—in his need to keep on coming. Even I tried to stop him. But the Sheriff's car came whining up and the Sheriff jumped out and got the boy in a bear hug. The others kind of fell off in the dark, Sheriff's boys made them get in their cars and trucks and drive on out. I looked in the red-domed station wagon and saw the boy laying on the back seat clutching his arm, his face gone the color of mustard. "Git on home now, sonny-boy. Y'hear!"

I came up on our house from behind. We had a long, tapered backyard, topped by a big rough oaktree and crossed, a few yards further down, by seven rows of peanut bushes dug in by my mother for reasons she kept, as always, to herself. I came and leaned against that tree. The stars were still bright but the breeze had died completely.

I saw it then, without at first even knowing. In the tree above, in perfect stillness, two high branches moved. Starlight flickered through to me, diverted from its possible random path. I had almost not seen the leaves of the tree move. But I did see, and a glow fanned out within me; my skin tingled all over, fingers and toes twitched, head near explosion with sudden full rush of blood. It seemed that something had come to me, a gesture, from the earth, the air, or beyond. I'd had a sign. I'd had a sign then. The night-tree-stars enveloped me. I smelt the wine-rich woodsmell mingle with odor of mucky earth. I leaned dizzily against the trunk, a little frightened, and an odd high patch of moss pressed soothingly against the chafed skin where the tear exposed my shoulder. It was all right, it was going to be all right. I drew a deep breath, my burden lifted. I cried for joy—and capered in the peanut rows.

And here I sat in the empty fountain, remembering clearly, for the first time, what I suppose I'd taken all along for granted. A load of horseshit! Give me back my burden, Lord, and I'll return to thee thy cunning little sign. Or give me another one, better than the other one. . . .

The trouble had begun (or continued) right away. As I pranced inspired in the peanuts, already tugged by that first faint tinge of exhaustion, I saw the black shape of my father loom out of the dark back near the house. I fell flat, too late: he lumbered unsteadily towards me.

"Alex fella! You out here? I know it's you, fella!"

He hove up large as a house in the faint-lit darkness. Then tripped foot-tangled in the tuberous bushes, fell heavily down in the trough where I lay.

Nose to nose I glared steely and unflinching in my father's face. Let him break my arm then, if the fates would have it. He opened his mouth—and drooled. He was drunk; he stunk of Kansas wheat-whiskey.

"Saw you out here," he said. "Thought it was . . . someone."

I didn't say a word.

"Young fella, you listen to your papa." You could have heard him breathe for miles. "There's been time and money invested up to your ears." Breathe, breathe. "And damn little respect!"

The ugliness was overwhelming. I scrambled up a furrow, about to run, when he caught my ankle and left me clawing at the loose soil.

Next thing I knew he'd flung his bulk on top of me, anchoring me among the barely-sprouting peanut plants.

My knee was twisted under, and I cried out, but the old man didn't hear; he lay like a dead weight, wheezing. I pressed my face in the sandy clay. I could endure. I'd lie there till he died, if need be.

I heard him babbling, wheezing, moaning while I cursed to myself and waited. Finally some words got through:

". . . trying to tell you, trying so damn hard. I'm sorry son, I'm really sorry."

With that the old man shut up, stopped wheezing, almost stopped breathing. But I couldn't get out from under. And damned if I would make a gesture or say one word. I wished to hell I were across the sea, in London, in Shanghai, standing in a tower, leading a parade of troops, addressing the entire people.

Near me a little bush had put out its first flower, a yellow jewel the size of a pea. With my free hand I squeezed the bud between thumb and forefinger. It would open wide at sunrise, wither by noon. In a day or two the flower stalk would begin to grow, elongate to a stemlike peg. Its tip would swell with seed, grow downward a foot or more, push its head into the soil and mature down under to a god-bless peanut pod. My mild ironic mother would dig it up then, crack it absent-mindedly and pop the little brown nuts into her mouth.

I can see it even today, the clearest object in that long blurred night.

A chilly wind sprang up, sweeping loose soil along the ground and into my nose and eyes.

"Alex," my father said. I knew I'd never answer. But the man was about to say more, and he must at all costs be stopped.

He rolled a little, the weight was unbearable. He was struggling to clear his throat and head.

"Okay! Okay!" I whined. I'd begun to wriggle violently. "I got to go—let me out of here!"

I clutched at the furrow, my mouth pasted with a sudden dirtclod. I spat frantically. *"Okay!"*

The weight lifted quickly; my father was ten yards away before I could stir to see him, walking fast, not like a drunk man, stepping evenly and not looking back.

What can I tell you? My happy memories were blasted, thank god, by an earth-shaking roar. As the noise faded I was overrun by the inner population, who ran screaming and freaking into the backyard. Halleluyah they raised their hands on high to where an oldtime biplane wheeled against the sun, passed through a low cloud, and turned for another run at the house. "It's Dr. T., on a wing and a prayer!" I had a glimpse of Tyrtan's manic face as he buzzed the house again—and pulled up at the last second. He wore a black jacket and Nelson Rosenberg his co-pilot one very white lollypop!

Our congregation meanwhile fell and rose again, robes flapping in the breeze, cheering waving jiving to the power on high, imploring, some of them, for bombs. A turret window shot up and a Negress in a fez stuck out her head full of sunglint teeth. Others running on the roof fell flat as the bi-plane swooped belly low. And moviemakers yelped with pleasure while their precious footage whirred.

The cockpit was open and Tyrtan's wild laughter floated back to us as swop! he expertly flipped the creaking flapping sandwich over on its back. The sun was blotted by the passing plane and released again in a straight stab of light. I stood alone rubbing my eyes, an island of blindness in an ocean of raving seers. Wrong all wrong: twenty years, and I could not fly!

10

THE INWARD SWIRL had speeded up on me, events and people splintering in fragments which shot through my brain too dense and quick to get a fix on. The answer was sleep but a humming energy flowed through the walls and floors to intercept me. As the house prepared for dinner my pillow soaked up a cacophony of noises, like a hunk of electrosponge amplifier.

I jerked up, eyeballs automatically clicking along preset circuits in the vine-twisted tapestries. In the corner of the screen, a subliminal bi-plane pierced the curve of my little window and settled to earth in a groove beyond.

Don't know whether I dozed or simply sunk to a feebler state of being. But after a time I could neither sleep nor measure—and the soft flapping walls began to move in. I would shut my eyes, only to see the lids swoon up in a weak terror. The black insides of my vision were like the shutters of a box. I had to run outdoors from myself, to a high open place, but my body was anchored; I couldn't make the break.

In the dark the Asians might creep like roaches to seize my every member, rope ankles tight to neck. With tiny forks they'd peel at membrane holding in my eyes. Perhaps they'd already begun, with Billy. Try to concentrate: was Billy taken? Listen to your nerve tip endings.

Silence there. But I knew for sure my brother was theirs—and that he paid in pain for every dollar and second of my useless existence.

I had blacked out for a space, but a pulse of energy shot through me and twitched me out of bed. I dove for the draperies, pushed them flat against the wall. Threw open the window to early stars in the sky, lights shining in another wing of the house. I shook my limbs and jangled up and down. I was weak; it took all I had to establish location.

Ready at last to face dinner I stuffed keys and wallet back in their compartments, but stopped short as I scooped up the change. *Suppose the Drug were your last hope?* I flipped up a quarter and watched it settle in the fibers of the floormat, showing not our country's father who could not tell a lie but an eagle with wings spread like a wall to say No, tails, thou shalt not pass. I snatched it again and flipped it up in the narrow shaft of light, where it spun off a shower of sparks from the dying sunset.

There was a baby under the table. Once in a while it clutched my pants, and I reached down to rub its head and try to smooth the baffled look from its face. Above board our whole crew sat banqueting, a regular bourgeois ceremonial, with Father Tyrtan gazing enraptured into his goblet. "Extraordinary," he mused, "how a range of social values attaches to each wavelength of the spectrum."

Ah they looked too, into the depths of their ruby goblets, and as they did Dr. Tyrtan glanced down the table looking for me with that grin, as if to say, dig these crazy people!

He had the air of a potentate, leaning back, expanding visibly as the Negro cook put before him a tray of figs and dates and nuts in honey. He was dressed in a black suit with sparkling white shirt open at the collar: a perfect set-off for his brilliantly flaring hair. Now and again he reached under the table to flick a switch—and the music would jump from Bach to electronic to serial to raga to bossa nova bonkbonk. You could see the eaters jerk, as if they were plugged in to the pre-amp.

Nelson Rosenberg was frowning again, possibly at me, but a camera was projecting beautiful gentle color film of Blonde Star all over him and the wall behind. "You scrumptious thing!" I called. He looked to see himself on simultaneous TV and quickly got out from under. And Nina left too, very quietly, having not once removed her shades. But the rest of them were having a ball. They chattered away of scores and scenes and groovy dreams, knowing full well a tape-recorder was coming along rebroadcasting three minutes behind, a loop of time returning steadily and wrongly but in all new cadence.

"Time and space," said Seymour; "to break beyond that bag," and so on; but the tape had him in a low croon of Illinois moonlit island summerair icecream. Tyrtan switched channels and eight ghostly voices throbbed, *my world is empty without you, babe.* And all us boys and girls were bathed in Alaskan travelogue: walls of snow, cascading waters, pickets of pine on the horizon. Johnnie snapped a picture of Amber and me and produced it on the spot. Couple from Iowa sprawling at New Year's shindig. Flypaper streamers descending with song of dying flies. And a cumquat popped between her lips. Pass to the right from communal mouth to mouth: winner eats all. Grieg fell down a flight of stairs; Beethoven fumed; raga turned all into very thin dew, and yet. . . . Twenty slides of Tyrtan all in white sitting lotus-position swelling enormous till he burst into fountains of white carnations tumbling from every wall and disappearing with sudden blowout of the slide projector. "My man!" says Seymour. Smear this nice jelly, smile purple for the folks at home. Jacky holds microphone flush against palate, coming to you now through courtesy of foundation for the culture of culture center grant. "Now this here's greasy kid stuff Hi Mom—" A session-session-session, they whispered, going on in Piero's room.

And when all was cleared away and machinery mailed in for processing, then, most of all, was family hour and time for the heap of Sunday Village Post in the middle of the table. With happy cries we dug our sweaty hands into a pile of freeswinging tough impressionistic up-to-date material, and began to pull out juicy plums of just what everyone needs. The best of it was we could laugh laugh while we dug dug, because we were hip, dig, it was understood.

One of the models read word by word expressionless: "The soft drink with a message: tingling tartness. The sound of Trite is a real taste quake. Switched on. Exuberant. Noisy."

And I read much too eagerly, "Don't be afraid to speak out! Now a powerful new mouthwash bolsters the courage of rebels everywhere," boyish offkey but the newsprint was flying like shredded shrapnel and no one noticed maybe.

Strike a blow for Originality! Join the Fashion Rebellion! Join the Sex Revolution! Join the Molecular Carnival! The Experience is Color! Has Monogamy Failed? One critic wrote I ought to try an analyst. Drastic Techniques of Achieving Freedom. Talk softly . . . and wear a Gentleman's Cologne. (Hosting a Rabelaisian Romp.)

"Tom's ambition," said a friend, "is to know everyone of his time who is famous or interesting. He wants to make his life a work of art."

Come as you are—in last year's face. Fashions for the Youthquake: a tribute to the tormented comedian who exploded standup monologue into biting satire and scathing social commentary. He makes it at school or on the surf, at a happening or the flicks: a whole other scene! International hangouts for the young nomad set—from Agadir to Ahmadnagar. One way to say you're there: fab swim caps of kicky printed knits! After breast surgery: a Playboy panel on Religion and the New Morality. The strip's most impressive freak-rock contribution takes refuge on the Lower East Side! In the Fervor of Orthodoxy he sought Surcease from Temptation; on the Day of Atonement his Wish for Saintly Celibacy was Shockingly Fulfilled! It Works! he cried, I've Graduated from Dandruff! Acting Classes for "In" Teenagers. A turned-on Scene with Techniques, Improvisations and Psychodrama specially for YOU! Whoever you are! Lettice Greene, Movie Face with a Future. The '64 Girl! Tuned in. Connected. Moving. Whippy. Flamboyant. Zero Cool.

Despised. Loved. Persecuted. Admired. Was he Sick or was Society? Falling in love is easy; true acceptance often a good deal harder. Do you have what it takes to join the Underground? Black Piranha—The Man's Deodorant. If you would like more information on Heaven, Hell, Purgatory, the end of the world and the resurrection to follow . . . we shall be happy to send you a pamphlet. Nobody will call on you.

Have you tried coral the kickiest side of the Color Explosion? Have you tried Man's Destiny by leading scientists? Have you tried the New York nitery with a new-sound Nashville Nottingham music mix? Have you tried AWARENESS? Have you tried THE SUPRA-CONSCIOUS? Have you tried Pani Plotzfleisch and his no-nostalgia nightclothes for neo-romantics? Have you tried the Loveable Heel, shapely and high-rise? Have you tried guerrila warfare? (Which side are you on, babe?) Have you tried the wonder drug acetylcholine an alkaloid obtained from ergot for subliminal blood pressure and groovy peristalsis? God wants us to be Happy and Free! But have you ever tried? Have you tried have you tried HAVE YOU EVER TRIED. . . .

"My guesties!" Headlights swept through the French windows; Mona Sweetan danced happily to her feet. She and Jacky Mayflower rushed outside to greet a squadron of limousines. Meanwhile Seymour was passing out new equipment. Outside the ladies and gentlemen disembarked and followed their welcomers through the dark back passageway into the house and into the long hall . . . *to be greeted by a row of rubber masks!*

The chandelier had been turned off and by flickering taper-light our furred visitors could see the silent shadow-faces of their culture's unreal mask people. Not a sound could be heard as they looked from one rubber face to the next. We had the world's great proclamators —and their brave consorts full of personality. The prophets of our time. Stars of the night and seers of a new day. Mind-benders. Movie money photo faces. Leaders of the people and people of the leaders. Comic strip magicians detectives dumbbells yokels victims mad scientists and enemies of aggression.

The well-bred guests shrank back in amazement, clustered together in their capes and overcoats. Jacky Mayflower gaped open to laugh but couldn't wheeze a sound. The rubber masks stared on in shrouded silence, judge and jury, fixed and relentless in passive eternal impossibility.

I couldn't take it; snatched off my Ghandi mask and

ploughed through the press. Behind me something shattered; voices broke out; someone ran after me.

I heard Seymour call as I reached the first landing of the broad front staircase. I hesitated, ran up a few steps, then stopped and waited as he came huffing after.

He drew close, nearly belly-bumping, up where I could see his little eyes spread out enormous on the octagonal lenses.

"You cutting out now?" he gasped, nodding his moon head hard with each word.

"Right!"

"Oh wow," he said. "I'm hip. I'm hip. But one thing . . . one word for you."

In the center of the eye-spread surfaces, his little pupils shone deadly hard and bright.

"Don't imagine . . . for a second . . . that you know."

"What?" I said. But I had heard him.

"You don't know . . . anything."

"What the fuck you mean?" I shot out.

"Huh!" He snorted in ineffable contempt, stepped back a step. Then a sly smile stole across his head. He'd thought of something. "Okay man," he said. "Come on." He backed down a few steps. He beckoned with his pillow neck.

I followed down along the sweeping stairs, through a short passage and into a closed chamber beneath the staircase.

"Feel."

The room was tight and dark. Seymour held out . . . what? Two curved rods half-hidden by his bulk. I reached, and saw his face contort with inward cunning. I had put my hand on the chopped-off forepaws of the deer. "Too much," he crooned. With disarming gentleness he thrust the paws against me, his tender fat hands folding my own about them. I stood thus, mouth and nostrils fouled with essence of carrion, fingers crawling with dry blood, anger paralyzed in softness.

I dropped the paws and pushed away the weakly giggling jello. But as I passed he flopped against me from behind and draped his heavy arms about me, splashing his lips in my burning ear. "Puke, baby." My knees were buckling; I lurched, mashing him against a wall; felt the loose flesh wipe along my back. The arms were draining; they clung like rotten vegetation as I staggered into the hall. Dr. Tyrtan was waiting there in his black silk suit, elegant, surprised, disdainful, efficient. He slapped Seymour two quick slaps across the face and Seymour fell loose like a fibrous peeling. He seeped back into the hallway, leering, nodding. "I dig," he mumbled. "A groove." His head hung forward, nodding dripping, as he backed off into the dark.

"You have a way of getting into things," Tyrtan remarked.

"And now you'll see my way of getting out."

"Then you're leaving?"

"Unless you want to turn me on," I said in sarcasm.

"All right," he said politely.

"Don't put me on," I said.

He said nothing.

"You told me you never gave drugs," I said.

"So I did."

We looked at each other.

"But that was because . . ." I trailed off.

"Because I had no right to trust you," he finished. "I am responsible for a great many others. I make very few exceptions, Alex."

"Then I'm an exception?"

"I knew that from the moment I saw you."

"Well," I said. I laughed a brief unnatural laugh.

"The point is," said Dr. Tyrtan, "I do trust you."

I turned away in some confusion. Because I felt so fine. . . .

"Shall I leave you?" Tyrtan asked.

"No—that won't be necessary." There was nothing to think about. You can't stop halfway in.

"When?" I said.

"We'll make our contract for midnight tonight. Our visitors will be gone by then. You ought to go to your room now and stay quiet. I won't offend you by suggesting meditation."

We nodded coolly; we understood.

I didn't want that room or any other confinement; I wandered, returning to a door I'd seen at the end of my corridor, beyond which a set of narrow stairs wound round a pillar and up into a tower. I could sense as I climbed the opening-out at the top, the expansion of air, the sudden pushing-back of space as my foot missed an imaginary step and I realized myself in the middle of a dark room. I turned, groping with my senses, and found not light but a pocket of new dark mixed with subtle reflections where a long window fronted the sky. A tiny idol sat beneath, with a tiny candle in its gut, perhaps the captured center of that invisible sphere whose outer arc was dotted by the winkings of numberless stars.

As my eyes widened I made out a silent form sitting in repose on a kind of platform by the side of the window.

"Who is it?" I whispered.

I felt no motion in reply, not a breath, not a stirring. . . .

A match—and I recognized Nina, whose hair lay in rich wings folded neatly about her oval face.

"I'm sorry," I said. "I didn't mean—"

"That's all right," she said quietly.

She lit a larger candle.

"Dr. Tyrtan said I could walk around, and I . . ."

"I see," she said.

It occurred to me she might have been her twin sister.

"Are you you?" I asked. "Or are you someone else?"

"I am," she said.

Should I talk to her? Sit next her on her bed? She met my gaze neutrally and calmly.

I did sit down!

"I guess this is, um, your room?"

"Yes," she said.

"And you're alone or is someone else . . . ?"

"My husband is in India."

"Excuse me," I said, most idiotically. It flashed through my mind that her husband was Vishnu.

"I'm bothering you," I said.

"No."

She was merely indifferent. Whatever she had, whatever she knew, she was keeping it cool and tidy beneath the wings of her calm head and the modest flannel of her pyjamas.

"You must miss your husband," I said. I no longer cared what I was saying.

"Oh no," she said.

"Seems silly to be here . . . on another person's bed . . ."

It was silly, but what could I lose? I reached for her.

"I'd like to lie down with you," I said.

"That wouldn't be too neat," she answered.

"Just thought I'd ask," I said, rising.

"That's all right," she said again.

"No it's not," I said; "it's really not." But she didn't respond and I retreated.

Then I did something I've always been glad for: broke out whistling, *Yankee Doodle*. I whistle badly, but with astounding virtuosity.

Still whistling inside I sat on a mat in the middle of the meditation room. I was perfectly ready and self-possessed, as I'd been before big football games when I knew I would play as well as anyone. Light and heat from the fireplace stroked pleasantly across my face. Seymour and Dr. Tyrtan were making a fire. I liked to see them working. Before long they had logs blazing the entire length of the enormous fireplace, casting waves of smoky light across the big empty room with its rows of draped mattresses. The dark-paneled sidings of the room were darting with boomerangs of light from the mirror on the back wall. The phonograph played a stately baroque fugue.

Seymour started to seat himself, but Dr. Tyrtan plucked his sleeve. "I have a single contract with Alex," he said. "You'll be upstairs with Nelson."

Seymour turned abruptly—he had never looked at me—and left the room in that stiff-legged puffed duck walk of his.

Tyrtan and I sat facing one another, feet drawn up in the oriental manner. His black coat lay neatly folded on the mattress behind him. He ran his fingers up inside his suspenders, snugging them just so, and carefully set his hands to a sealed container. The man panted softly; his fair skin gave out a moist, rosy glow.

At his beckoning I held out my palm, into the flesh of which he dropped a heart-shaped pill. The Answer! I could have shouted out a great vulgar laugh. Then too, I thought of crushing the pill in my hand and throwing the powder over my left shoulder. Coolly I passed that moment by and put my hand to my mouth. Another pill passed into the mouth of Dr. T.

We clicked wine-glasses in a perfect delicate rim-to-rim clink. We drank, tipping back our heads. We bowed, ever so slightly.

Tyrtan swept his arm toward two mattresses in front of the fire. Side by side we stretched in wordless understanding, and lay relaxed, waiting for the blood to take hold of the chemical and sweep it upward to the brain.

Thus twenty minutes passed.

11

"OH MY DELIRIOUS BODY, baked into a pie!"

And when the pie was open, I was twisting and turning in rapture, singing softly in the harmony of a luscious spin: and the walls, the fire, the ceiling, the sky, all centered in, focused, and spun lushly about me.

Dr. Tyrtan sat up woozily, grinning in uncontrollable delight. It took great effort for him to bring his book, his manual, into his hands and read from it.

"Hear O sacred one!" (That was me!) "You are now setting out upon a voyage which thousands have traveled before you, since the beginning of time. A few remarkable men like Christ and Buddha have succeeded in bringing back something of what you are now about to experience."

"Experience?" More than that! Flat on my back I saw swirling clouds drift thickly, like premonitions of tornado, but thicker, richer, with edges locking in never-ending combinations. I drew them closer, closer; I was drifting between, flying myself like an airplane.

I moaned for the very joy of it. "O. O." Everything I said would at last be simple. "The heavens are opening. I can see! As though a great hand were pulling back the darkness . . ."

Thrillingly, from high above, the clouds began to part. It was too good, I wanted to keep it before me, to save it, which I could effortlessly do by opening my eyes.

Dr. Tyrtan was still with me, looking the same as always. But he was terribly terribly happy! And I knew why! I was happy for him!

"It's as you said," I told him. "Just like you promised. So beautiful beautiful. . . . I see it, certainly I see it, only. . . ."

(ages swoop)

"Only what?" he said.

"Only . . . I don't know if I can bear it. Bear such . . . happiness. I need you now. You mustn't leave me. I need you to tell me what I see."

"I'll be right here," he said. The pleasure, the deep relief, to hear those words! I sank back luxuriously on my mattress.

A few minutes later I opened my eyes, closed them, opened again. "It's happening!" It was truly happening. Every time I closed my eyes the unfolding resumed exactly where it had never left off. "And then when I open, I return. I'm on all levels at once. Whoops!" For it was happening now with my eyes open, the layers of surface peeling back in incredible richness.

The visual scene slid before me like divided pictures when the film is jammed. Inside, the same thing. I could go from the world of clouds, the higher drifting and pulling back, which I was saving for later—to the place back here where I was myself and taking it all in—to what was supposedly around me, the environment and myself inside it. But there was a potentiality to shoot out from the top. When I opened my eyes I was waiting, checking, delaying with relish my ultimate departure. The levels—I understood that—and the detachment, the something else. Words bound to be inadequate. The real thing lay behind, within: I had it too now, for my own sweet savouring.

Easy to see there had to be something if all the others went on talking and talking. And here it was, as I had known all along inside me it would be. All very natural, even my distrust. So right, as far as it goes, to distrust appearances. But back inside, deep around, could anything ever be other than natural? No more greater or lesser existences—all that fell away like a cankerous growth. Little earth full of canker. When you traveled, simply left that little earth, you saw again that everything simply *is*—as I had known and known and known.

The clouds were streaked with electric lines of infra-color. Paintings of a master mind. Here was the logic of abstract expressionism, made up retroactively by myself! I had started it all, so there could be no doubt that everything in the mind of man had its logic. I could see that now. And I opened my eyes to the mandala on the ceiling, letting it revolve in a counterswirl against the revolution of the room and the objects in it, spinning back against the movement of the earth and orbiting of planets to bring all matter-mirror-imaged with anti-matter, motionless in absolute neutrality, so that I myself might be sucked upward into a spaceless, perfect vacuum.

If I followed the delicate glottal stalks of the mandala, I would lose the clouds and the climb up to heaven. But my body expanded in luxury: I could afford to wait. I would come back and go out again. Just like the Blonde Star in her cosmic polkadots, sweet child of flesh and time, going in and out of her half-built house, passing back and forth over her threshold—*now I go in, and now I go out*—in her simple radiant belonging-to-things. So would I pass over my threshold, a million times or more inseparable one from the other, numberless and impossible to number, all life the passing in and out of soulstuff.

"There are certain souls," I murmured, "who can communicate . . ." The word *communicate* meant more than I could say. ". . . even in their earthly embodiment." Now how did I know that? Yet it was so. "But oh so imperfectly!" I moaned. A disaster here on earth, yet why be sad? The whole situation was exquisitely funny. Dr. Tyrtan was laughing. Someone was laughing—and many others. We all knew how to laugh. For once, I didn't resent it. Resentment all over with now. What a fool I had been! But that was the juiciest joke of all: I was far, far from a fool, the farthest of anyone, farthest ever. I had played it to the limit, all for a purpose. The limit had now been exceeded in the proper course of time happening, and soon the purpose would be known.

The little stalks waved inward as they circled, bending ever softly, weaving fine webs of tender inner flesh lips. I set my eyes between them, and softly sweetly spun on through, feeling their pulpy goodbye caress slide by as I gave myself to the vortex and let it draw me out through the bottom top.

He saw himself there, on the spread on the mattress on the floor in the room of the house. Saw himself from above, from the other side. Strong-looking high-cheekboned blond-haired boy, smile of idiot grace, lying for once arms and legs and belly wide open to beams of energy action love and hate. Goodbye Alex Randall!

A touching farewell! Not everyone could have managed it.

Sailing beneath textured cloud-ceiling. Not like clouds we know of this poor period but woolish gummy, oozing organic chromosomes, endless stretch of impenetrable riches. Flying flying with greatest of ease, shedding creeping undulation shadow upon the surface of the planet, winding over hills and lakes and trees. Deep black gulches way off on the edge, can't be seen as the shadow moves like magic over seas and lands and lakes. Now and there a molten bubbling of the surface. Ages slipping back, copper, iron; hairy animals bolten mubbly, bulk one another; jungles of leather birds and writhing reptile-tubes. Surface in a myriad of boiling molten eruption splashing down a fiery rain. . . .

Sailing, sailing over a bounding main of barren hot red clay. Flying over on a dead level, no past or future, fading steadily into an evenly-receding horizon line where the ceiling of sky meets the grey strip of earth. Flying just the same over volumes of water, waves falling equally in white lines, distributed, failing over and reforming, getting just as close just as fast to the horizon-end of nowhere. . . .

From far below a stirring, as Dr. Tyrtan heaves up an elbow. His face expanding in soft throbs, pulsing with heavenly glow. How beautiful back here to see one lone man, making the effort so effortlessly to break through on the same level, even as I myself dropped without effort to hear the words he was about to bring himself to read.

A ponderous voice this time, back from the very beginning!

"O blessed wanderer,

The time has come for you to seek new levels of reality.

Your ego and the Alex Randall game are about to cease.

You are about to be set face to face with the Clear Light.

In the ego-free sphere, wherein all things are like the void and cloudless sky,

And the naked spotless soul is a transparent vacuum."

What crummy poetry! Truly it was to laugh! But I could be all-generous. The truth was there, it had begun already. And I could laugh with the fullness of it, knowing myself indeed an apprentice.

"Am I silly?" I whispered.

"Not at all," he whispered back, between teeth locked in pleasure-spasm. He squeezed my wrist like a loving snake-band. Oh to think of him lying there, clutching teeth and hand like sphincters in his ecstasy, and myself, myself, it was all exquisitely. . . .

"Silly! Perfectly Silly!"

"Divinely Silly!"

We laughed with voluptuous delight! Knowing so well what we meant.

Where was my self then? Gone, blessedly vanished, no longer even remembering the name of the person who was the I of me. But that something, that something of a something, had had it told to him from way back and way deep that he was to be set, now, with the face of him to face the face of the Clear Light. And to do this the sky was cloudless. There in the Void beyond all clouds.

Drinking in the blueblack sky, lacy clouds streaking by now as my jet-rising soul ascended. Up in the high drift, black void space receding, wisps of cloud spreading, trailing . . . *pierced here and there by pinpricks of intense light! Each prick a stab of clear pure ecstasy!* Absent then all hot-cold light-dark odor-color-shape-form-matter-texture, joy-pain: all gone, like air from my old balloon, nowhere, nohow, no ma'am, nothing! No here no now no time no space no waiting! No seeing feeling touching tasting hearing. Washed in the soul of the light of the lamb of the lord. Prick! Flash! None of that! The surest thing he knew. (Then.)

Moaned a pleasure moan, couldn't get enough of it.

Because the clouds were in the way. Wisps of cloud flapping by the other way now, from the rear. I was receding. Still a prick—then no more. I hadn't got all the way to it. It was there, I had been shown, but I'd had only pieces. Got up close where no beginner had ever begun, only to slip back again. It came on and stabbed and stabbed but it did not stay; I could not get the whole of it. I could not get all the way up to it and into it.

I wanted to try so hard! But just then the blackness *spread,* terrifying, like a tent, like a great God-hand reaching over and pulling the curtains tight, closing it off, closing it all up!

I opened my eyes.

"I can almost," I said. "But I can't quite hold onto it."

"Don't force it," my doctor told me. His own eyes were closed. "Let it come."

Clouds drift thickly now in piles of white cumulus. Rather pretty: I could set my foot and walk, little prince on a stroll through his fluffy sky garden, black only around the edges. Down with that black! Back! Away from it! I would walk straight along the upward stairs and never stumble, never fall over into that treacherous reaching blackness.

You see! "It's like Dante!" I cooed. The clouds drifted deep into heavenly corridors, lined by fluted columns stretching in two endless rows. I came in slowly, gliding through fog-wisps as I settled for a landing on the cottony cloud carpet. I walked every step lighter, finer, losing all substantial weight but expanding in mass, in light energy, as I moved up that celestial corridor. Breath-takingly onward the columns pointed, to a mist-shrouded infinity. And back there, up there, at the end of the tracks, lurked the source, the answer, the light of lights. . . .

Already my feet dragged heavily. The pillars were above me once more, obscured again in fogs, fading from view. I was below the corridor, slipping backwards, and further below were clouds befouled with grey, and winds to suck me down again to the realm of matter.

And woe of blackness beckoned, a suffocating black gulch spreading like ink on a blotter. . . .

I sat bolt upright. "I'm not worthy!" I cried. "I'm not worthy to see the Clear Light! I go higher and higher but just as it begins the blackness comes and sucks me towards the pit!"

"The pit isn't real," murmured Dr. Tyrtan. It was marvelous, I could see, the effort to force his words out, absorbed as he was in a long-practiced ecstasy all his own.

"Only the light is real. . . ." he said.

I flopped back content. How could I not be content? There was nothing else but now. And I had seen so much, and felt so good. Wasn't it all a bit thick, I mean stylistically? But I could laugh at all that now. Everything was as it should be, and I was far above my usual pathetic trifling. I knew that when I returned my earthly life would be sheer tonic. I was full of blissful gratitude. There was nothing more to sweat about back there, no question of demand or disappointment. I would be able to wait and wait. Because I knew I had it now. I lay eyes open, watching the firelight flicker on the walls in luscious explosions of green and yellow. For me—the signs were all for me!

"And one of these days," I moaned, "I will see the Clear Light. Not yet—but some . . . time, some . . . guise, some . . . incarnation!"

Chuckles bubbled in my throat, roses of vaporous delight.

"Alex," said Dr. Tyrtan. "You're so beautiful. You're beautiful, Alex. If you could only see yourself!"

"But I've not yet found my true power!"

"You're doing well. You're doing fine. I knew you would from the very first moment. Your face shone out to me."

"But if only . . ." I had to struggle for words. My own personality was so laughably pitiful.

"It's just that what I've bothered being . . . all I

could be, I suppose, granted . . . everything . . . is the tag end of myself. What I show, what others see . . . is just the tag end. I'm not worthy . . . I see that now. I'm not worthy of all that's been put into me. So much there, inside . . . but I can't hold it. . . . I'm not adequate. I'm a flawed vessel."

"And does it bother you?" He was so gleeful!

I had to laugh. "Of course it doesn't bother me! Nothing bothers me. And you know that! What devilish fun you must have, with a person like me! Yes, you know what you're doing. Everything you say is for a purpose. And it must be fun!"

"For a purpose?" he needled.

"No purpose—you know what I mean. Because there is an incredible vision, a oneness. It isn't just a matter of believing, is it? Because it explains too much. . . ."

I trailed off, but by and by I heard him asking, "What does it explain?"

"Everything!"

I was absorbed by a vision of color taking place inside my eyelids. An orgy of mutant shapes reveling through pastures of the spectrum. A good time later I opened my eyes and found Tyrtan sitting up and watching me.

"You don't know what it is just to look at you," he said.

It was my turn to laugh at him.

"You'd better be careful!" I warned. I seemed to know all sorts of things. "Don't forget I understand your motives too! All those bits of yours, the things that disturbed me—yes, they *should* have disturbed me! Even you are inadequate. You've been given much, but you're still what you are. Or you're struggling to be. All of us . . .

struggling. We are only . . . incarnations of ourselves. And we have to . . . strive."

Dr. Tyrtan sighed a mellifluous sigh, stretched lazily over onto his stomach. "Strive, Alex? Does the flower strive to open to the sun?"

"No, no." I was weakly laughing. "Words so inadequate. That's the poison in me, words, thoughts. It all comes from reading! I'm so English you know. Want to see words lined up in English syntax. Syntax a fraud. Syntax strives. My people all strived, my father. And that was me striving. Striving in the paper bag of my ego. No real opposition between me and my Daddy—more invention of the ego. I can see my father sitting at a desk. And I see myself. His face is my face. I can see that face fade back through the ages all the way to Britain. I see the face on top of a wall . . . throwing things down on people . . . people trying to get up. Great wall of mud . . . see them slipping and sliding. See that face in a mask of armor . . . You know, it was a noble face. Knightly. But what happened? Not that it matters. Even faces don't matter. . . ."

I faded again. "Faces are illusions, masks, games," intoned my guide.

". . . and to fight," I droned. I lay relaxed now, one step down from the charge of ecstasy. "No, my dear, dear, dearest father. I don't want to fight you. I hate you because I hated me, I wanted to get rid of me. Lose myself, be someone else's son. Son of a stranger, left there with uncouth people. Because I couldn't do away with the uncouthness that was me. . . . I fought you to kill myself. And in loving you now I embrace for the first time all that I have ever been and will ever be. . . ."

I embraced myself tightly, tenderly.

"Son of a stranger! Oh it was true! And the stranger

is you, and the stranger is me, and the stranger is God, and the stranger is this strange man right here!"

"Am I a strange man?" Dr. Tyrtan murmured. "Many think so."

"Well they're right!" I said. "Let's hear no more about it!"

We laughed and laughed.

"You're lovely Alex, your eyes are wide open, you've gone exploring and you don't need a map," said Dr. Tyrtan some time later.

I lay still hugging myself, eyes clamped tight.

"You'll make your own map," he said.

I could see without looking his hands floating high and wide, like doves in the belfry of a cathedral. He was in truth reaching towards me, his fingers making plucking motions as though I were a flower. But I had no petals, and he was miles, miles away.

His voice came unencumbered. "What do you think now of that body of yours?"

The time-lag filtered my reply from space to space.

"My body is your body. Your body is my body. Body left far behind, no longer a problem . . ."

Opened again and there was Tyrtan kneeling before me. Which was all as it should be.

"Because," I said, "I am God."

I gazed simply and truly upon the man before me.

The man smiled wickedly. He was the Devil after all, though that made little matter.

"Everyone is God," the man said.

"That's true," I replied instantly. "Quite true. And rather amusing, when you think about it."

For myself, thinking was no longer necessary. Whatever was so, simply registered.

I began to pace around the room, each pace a continent. After some planning I paced two paces. "Only one problem," I announced.

Several eons further on he asked what was it, and I snapped back instantly to the required level. It would be lovely, I knew, to say what I was about to say, and Dr. Tyrtan would love me for it.

"My only problem . . . is"—balancing coyly in mid-pace—"should I go into energy?"

"Ah yes," Tyrtan said. We relaxed then; we could have vaporized if so we wished. But he made it to the turntable and put on a record of hand plinking strings. Impossible, irrelevant the style or form or period. Each note rose in its own shell of being, different from every other as grapes on a vine. One lingered, its skin fell away, and it came to my mouth round and succulent. Soon the next note squeezed itself to birth. I could see it rise, lustrous and perfect, from the surface of the record. Mozart, I knew, by the shape of it, and rarity of notes in a cluster. And by the keen dry taste of it, the coolness, the bouquet, the same amusement. . . .

I lay spreadeagled, limbs twitching as energy flowed through.

"Never mind never mind never mind," I said. "I've been here before. What is there to know? Why do I keep asking? It's all the same. I understand everything."

"Think about *understanding,*" said Dr. Tyrtan.

"Yes, it's not that, not that at all. It is, and I am, and I listen and hear it within me. So silly to worry about learning, knowing. *I am*—and that's everything! Descartes said that, didn't he? He knew."

"Wise men have always known," said Dr. Tyrtan. His legs were crossed; he was sitting calmly.

"And you must remember, Alex, don't let them

tell you it was all an illusion. Remember how I am with you. I know exactly where you are. If the Answer Drug were only a drug, as you believed when you came here, how could the two of us communicate so perfectly?"

I couldn't get over it.

"Oh what a fool, what a fool! Why I thought . . . I was the center of everything!"

"And now?"

"Everything is the center of me!"

I was telling him a story; the fabric of my talk spun out golden from my lips and mingled with light-fibers of the air. My childhood theory of atoms: how startled I'd been to learn that the solid table was made of particles, themselves containing mostly empty space. But I saw that the electrons revolved about the nucleus just as the planets of the solar system revolved about the sun. "Maybe then our whole universe is just a molecule in a world of titans. An air molecule that gets breathed in and out without our knowing it, part of something solid despite our sensation of spinning loose. It follows that even the smallest particle has life upon it, minute but self-enclosed, just as we are self-enclosed, with only the barest glimmers to hint at the larger order it is part of, or, if you can imagine it! the micro microcycle of life which its every sub-atom sustains. Thus the million atoms on my fingertip are a million solar systems, and our sun with all its planets, comets, satellites and asteroids is one of a million atoms on the fingertip of a still larger being. . . ."

Dr. Tyrtan remained silent, his eyes twitching behind closed eyelids.

"But that's not true, is it?"

He shook his head from side to side.

"It was only a pre-vision," I continued, "of the eternal oneness of everything. Things are not more separate than they seem . . ."

But I trailed off. I was losing it. The suction of the air was pulling the segments of my brain apart.

"All matter is illusion," Dr. Tyrtan incanted. "Only the Void is real. Only the Clear Light of the Void."

"Things are more unified," I said. "That is what I feel now, what I always knew, if only I could trust myself. Atoms must be whole; positives and negatives cannot exist apart from one another."

"That is all a bad dream of yours," said Tyrtan steadily. "Empty your mind of all subjects and objects. Don't try to think. Relax. Accept. Float downstream."

"But you're not with me now!" I wanted to rise, but my body remained where it was. Perhaps it didn't matter. "The positive and negative cancel each other," I said: "all is wholeness, and wholeness is spirit . . . substanceless spirit. Only . . . can everything really be nothing? I can't quite hold it in my mind. I'm afraid . . . it will slip away."

"The problem is merely of the mind," he chanted. "Forget your mind. Flow out, follow your yearning. The flow of life is passing through you, dazzling, harmonious, pure. Do not try to control or understand: flow with it. Come out from the ends of your nails and the fine hairs of your pores. Merge and flow; no need to think or act. You are absorbing the great lessons of creation, evolution and consciousness. If you try to stop the flow, you may fall into a hell of unbearable torture invented by your own poor limited mind. Void your mind of game-playing. Keep faith in the spirit-flow. Melt in the rainbow, the river, the everfecund oceantide. Trust your guide, enlighten yourself, and you may float downstream to the ecstatic liberation of Buddhahood. . . ."

I put the suggestion in my suggestion-box. Before long I was possessed by voices, singing in tongues long vanished from the human ken. My lips and tongue multiplied a thousand times, filling the room with little pockets of lip and tongue. The air was pouched into honeycombs, dripping blood, while little red hammers darted out of their centers to strike and suck at the flesh. And all the while I went on chanting my inspired babel, my throat an instrument through which ancient lore invoked itself. The little squares rotated, shifted pattern, tore silently apart and reassembled. Horizontal lines filtered down from floor to ceiling, vibrating and dividing in spectroscopic formations as I myself was sucked in among them, slipping in and out as I floated easily across the grain.

Sudden tentacles of blackness stabbing from a huge black cell. Panic! I veer sharply away like a fish.

"Can't catch me! Hoo ha ha! I'm gonna lay my eggs in that big old fresh-water lake!"

At that very instant I began to divide myself in lightning chain-reaction: and squealed our challenge in the seventh tongue of the seventh tribe to drive away the darkness.

Having divided down to the basic, I knew one perfect solitary moment of amoebahood. Single-celled and mindless I triumphantly surrounded a grain of food; nurtured it within like the yolk of an egg; ripened in the primordial soup till I was teeming with potential; exploded then to infinities of egg-atom-star-cell-eye.

The myriad particles of me percolated downward through the glueish primaeval air, in full slow pleasure, permeating all substance. We landed and ate into the earth in little pellets of living lunching fire. Then clustered in an allembracing spherical strip. Flaps cornered themselves and lifted, as I began to dissect the surface of myself into numberless flat sections each one rolling into a sun-size snowball of cosmic no-matter. We gave out fire from the bowels of our radiance, spat planets to revolve about us. Moisture collected, rain fell, trees grew, mighty oceans swept across our retinas. Once more the spinning-wheel of spacetime was reestablished. Soon I would divide myself down again, to arise an amoeba from the mucky bottom of myself.

My cosmic density forced my very eyes to bulge, like Dr. Tyrtan's only more so. With the power of those eyes I might shoot raw energy to burn to a cinder any hostile soul come eye-to-eye to question my cojones. But I could afford to forgive; for I was radiant with love, and irresistably lovable. My secret was my unstrained confidence. I sat at the center of myself, the source of all that would come to me. In my relaxation I let my mighty burning eyes plop out and bounce around with all their kinesthetic grace.

Soon the entire room filled with bouncing eye-balls, each pulsing with the warmth of a sun—rolling, rubbing, jumping, gyrating, counter-gyrating, kissing and squeezing for joy! Inside each glowing bouncing capsule crouched my own homunculus, with massive water-filled head, eyes closed and hairless, little rat-paws clutched about his up-drawn knees.

From a sweetsmelling shrine-lit corner of the womb floated a larger, paler ball, emitting a soft violet light. Inside sat Dr. Tyrtan, with feet drawn up and turban on his head, jeweled forebrow and soft baby belly of the bountiful Buddha. Inexorably the delicate Buddhaball drew near, revolving in its luminescent glow.

"You!" I spoke. The round word blossomed like a thunderclap. I broke from my capsule, which fell about me like the halves of an egg. Out I stepped, each step stately, foreordained, fitting in the feet of ancient footsteps.

"I see you at last," said I, "as I see you for the first time. I now know what I have seen and not seen every time I looked at you: the other half of me, the half denied but undeniable!"

Slowly the Buddha face blurred: a new face forming, face of me myself, smiling, laughing, beckoning in open revelation!

Hail, O destiny! Thus I hailed him: "The other half of the ocean, the mud, the slime, the stars! We are the two opposing forms of man, thinker and mystic, each yearning toward the other as the minus yearns toward the plus. Oh I could hate you! And you hate me! Deep down you wish me destroyed. You want to absorb me, and in so doing complete yourself. That is what was meant from the beginning, from the creation of all matter. Human history only the tag end of an eternal process we are destined now to fulfill, and to fulfill again, again and yet again. Our coming together was long ago foreseen and foreordained!"

—To all of which Dr. Tyrtan smiled his Buddha smile, as befits that Being who has seen all forms of existence manifest themselves in cycles of eternal vanity. . . .

I was crawling toward him. Though I worked with all my might, my body moved minutely, as if encased in densest plasma. Up and down walls I crawled, through searing fire, across burning deserts and the surface of a mighty river.

"We've come a long long way," I said. "Every event and person my whole life long directed me here to this room and to you."

"—And to the Drug, the Drug," he replied, looking like himself now.

I came crawling through boiling pearls, through gems. I saw him smile in lofty understanding. His lips rippled like water.

Much later I reached the edge of the mat where my guru waited. Humbly I pressed my lips to the dirty floor.

For a moment I gathered in, gulping deep draughts of air to quench for good and all pride's inner fires. Then bolted up, like a startled animal, flung violently forward to clasp his hand.

"We meet again!" I cried. "We meet again!"

12

My hand clasped tightly to the ringed pale hand of Dr. Tyrtan.

We lay parallel, head to toe, each with knees curled slightly and one elbow supporting the weight of his trunk. The fervor of my grip shook his arm to its roots; I could see him cautious in his smile. But I didn't care; I was putting everything I had into the final blending of the destined halves, which I knew as well now, or even better, than he did.

The clasped hands vibrated and went into a spin, our bodies trailing in a circle of yin and yang. From beyond the circumference came a sermon in my own inspired voice.

"You are the seducer, I the conqueror. Everywhere I push, you yield. We are Cain and Abel, Jacob and Esau, Achilles and Hector, Aeneas and Dido, Jesus and Mary, Dante and Virgil. . . .

"We are sultan and saint . . ." My own dear strong body clothed in opulent silks—while pitiful rags dangle from the weaker frame of Tyrtan.

". . . black and white . . ." Dr. Magus descends via helicopter into a clearing of grass-thatched huts. He bounces down squinting through a monocle, shaded from jungle sun by a pith helmet. Kneeling in naked blackness by his imperial shortpants, I bow my nappy forehead as a heavy chain is set around my neck. *Benedictus qui venit.* Soon he will distribute chewing-gum and opium. . . .

". . . mind and body . . ." I compress into a dense blue dot, as Tyrtan, liquifying, flows round and round about me.

". . . two life cells in the protozoic sea . . ." Hardly any room there! And the heaviness pressing down on us from above, binding us together!

". . . two particles at the node of the universe . . ." Superimposition of a pair of dust motes. An eternal tickle, each from the other: faint pure itch, never to be scratched. . . .

A throbbing one-note bass plucked at my ear as I faded upwards and outwards from the scene. First there were the two of us, curled like castor and pollux in our wet salt sack, then the House, with a faint light at the top where a ray from Nina's magic candle crept silently to the stars. I saw the pale green planet squeaking on its axis as it ground its way through space banded in halves by an equator. The earth grew smaller, and a silver pea popped out to become its moon. Out beyond the solar system I drifted, hearing weird faint wailings from farthest space, as the milky-way took shape and belted the visible horizon, only to fade to a coin, spinning among other galaxy coin-shapes head after tail as they receded.

Dr. Tyrtan's voice echoed from far away. "The Void . . . the Void . . . only the Void . . . only the Void is real . . ." He leaned over me, tightening his grip, bearing down. "The Void," he whispered, ". . . only the Void . . ." The string bass bombed bombed bombed its only empty boom. I had just then lost my last speck of light. I had receded to a point of utter black nothing. I groped for a moment in formless, spaceless, weightless absence. Then with a convulsive twitch I hopped the tracks for my return trip, threw off Tyrtan's hand and fell away in a spasm of terror. In the chamber of my head the spectral wailing reached its intensest pitch and broke off sharply; but the bass note throbbed on like the stroke of doom.

I'd scaled my ecstatic peak and fallen over on the downside. I bit my nails, I blinked. Random waves beveled and warped my field of vision. Static crackled across my eyeballs while floating spots of color exploded in sunbursts of tiny fragments.

At least I knew—what was it I knew? "I don't know," I mumbled. "So many levels . . . meanings . . . spaces. I'm not ready. I'm not ready for marriage. I hardly know . . . who I am anymore. Afraid. I admit it, but . . . it's true. So afraid . . . I might lose myself . . ."

"Nothing to lose, Alex. Forget space, forget meaning, forget losing and gaining. Just drop out, drift downstream."

"But I am afraid," I said. "I'm afraid I might *not* lose myself. So what difference does it make?"

I needed help—I had to turn to him.

"What if afterwards I feel this is all a deception?"

"That doubt is only the Alex Randall game playing itself once more. You will remember how we were together. You will never forget that."

"I'm not worried," I said, speaking from the top layer only of my skull. "I assure you I'm not. But it's so hard to know . . . where you are . . . or to find your way back. . . . Maybe I've been here before . . . and there will be some point . . . where it's all true. I can lose myself it seems . . . and I always come back. At least for now. But what if—"

"Alex! Look at the fire!"

The fireplace filled the entire room, Tyrtan and myself mere thumbkins on its hearthstone. Chinese walls of flame rose up, tossing like seawaves in a storm, bursting into whitecaps of color. Flowers leaped up on stems of foam and turned into bright soaring birds.

I heard myself cry out. "A fire, a fire, all my life, burning inside me. I remember, I remember now!"

"You have never forgotten," crooned Dr. Tyrtan. "It was in your head each time you turned to Plato. You recall the archetypal fire!"

"—Where souls return when they are freed of their bodies. Where they drink deep of all knowledge before they are born into forgetting!"

"Before they are born into a world whose apparent reality is only the shadows the fire casts on the back wall of a cave!"

"What was that?" I said. But the flames grew hotter and more menacing. Little red devils danced on the flickering flametips, popping their lips and brandishing pitchforks. In arrogant little leaps they began to spear the birds, which they roasted in a trice and devoured in smacking, slavering mouthfuls.

I couldn't watch. "My brain is boiling!" I cried. "I'm scared of . . . my own mind. It's flowing now and I can't stop it!"

My hysteria was mixed with a curious joy.

"Alex," said Dr. Tyrtan, "do you see now why we say, you have to go out of your mind to use your head?"

"Oh you bastard!" I said, but with a grin. What happy relief to have it all brought round! To submit at last to the clinching connection!

"And what do you know now about insanity?"

"That everyone's insane!"

"I dig that, Alex, that's a beautiful thing to say. Because everyone sees at best only a part of what you've glimpsed tonight. So-called insane people see a different part—usually a very fearful part—and so they're locked up. Because the society wants to tell you what you can and cannot learn about yourself."

"I don't care about myself," I protested. "All I care about is *it*."

"But you will have to go back," Tyrtan warned me. "You will have to decide how to make your re-entry and how you're going to play the game. You'd better take a look at your real self while you still can!"

"Oh God! Must I?" But I knew by now that no suggestion was mere accident. There was a path before me I had to walk—if I wished to come out on the other side.

I pressed my fists into my itching eyes. A young man was walking down a city street, glancing at every passerby a look of hidden want. Again, at his desk, reading, making notes, snatching in vain at supposed treasures in books. Or talking to his girl—so sincerely!—and yet with pain. With other girls—all lies. Seen from the scornful heights he moved through life a mechanical windup toy. Despite the agony of constant choosing, every act was pure reflex: walk sit read eat shit piss love talk sleep fight. . . . The grey light passing into his room, street outside with endless shoes and boots wearing down the snow. . . . Even in his boredom or his passion, so caught in what he was, so common.

"Too much, too much. It hurts too badly!"

And again without accident, Dr. Tyrtan had got to the turntable. In the helpless sky of my brain there soared a little chocolate bird with dark glasses, looping high and wailing. He moved among the golden lightning of the sunken sun, floating just where clouds were brightening, running on in unbodied joy. And the sound that poured forth, effortless moonrays, far beyond all human hate and pride and fear! Soon the roof of Heaven was criss-crossed with the hard bright crystal tracing of one lone bird; and I marveled, from my languorous dream, at the absolute spacing of his song. How I wondered what white thoughts were his as he shot like an arrow across the blue deep! Now he curled in a series of perfect tails; now he cried—in a sorrow beyond all tears. And ever and always, he knew where to put it and where to leave it alone, blowing his threads through velvet intervals of no-sound space. Oh if I could have that sense, could be that single chocolate bird! But I wasn't—I couldn't!

Teach me, I cried, half that gladness that your brain must know—let me hang it all together in a spaced-out, burning flow—then all these cats would listen—and everyone would know!

But he was gone gone gone—past the meadows, over the still stream, up the cloud-bank, lost forever in a valley of stars. Gone was his music—did I wake then or drop to waking sleep?

All I had left was Dr. Tyrtan lofting his slippered feet into a backstand Yoga position.

And more than ever, the puniness of me. He who needed the Drug to have a really freewheeling vision of himself! And yet the Drug made the dead reality I'd fled from all the more apparent, and hopeless, and impossible to put up with.

"Always thought I was smart. Thought I had skills . . . certain skills . . . no one else quite the same . . ."

"Everyone has the same skills," said Dr. Tyrtan promptly.

"Not exactly the same!"

Replied my mentor, contemplating his lofted feet: "Exactly the same!"

"You mean . . . they're not real? None of the things we do are real in any sense? Only this, now, with the Drug . . . only this is real?"

"Alex," said Dr. Tyrtan, "I think you could really

see yourself now. If you want to look. The mirror, my friend, the mirror!"

The long mirror still hung along the far wall, shimmering like a lagoon in the eerie light of the dying fire. I plunged toward it, and it gushed out to me in an ocean of liquid reflections. I swam forward with mighty strokes against the tide, aware that Dr. Tyrtan looked on floating in the background, propping his head with one hand, horizontal and at his ease.

The ocean vanished, sucked to an inner depth, leaving me frozen against the mirror, staring raptly to see my own face. But it was far away, at the end of a tunnel, a vague spreading crosshatch of half-transmitted wirephoto. I would bring it closer and tune it in: I willed that power within me, willing to become the operator of my own psychic projector, daring at last to focus my own true picture.

Then I had it: a little boy, eyes shining, cheeks two roses, prancing up and down in his impatience to see and touch and hold. Carefully I squeezed out a halo over the boy's fine hair, or rather, an effulgence, a radiance of divine energy. "Basically, I'm good," I announced in satisfaction.

Tyrtan's voice came floating from miles away: "Of course you are good! Ev-er-y-thing is gooood!"

"I mean I'm all right," I said. "I'm alive." In the mirror I saw tears course from my eyes for the sweet open willing child who didn't know the shaming and the mockery that awaited him.

Watered by my tears, a dark beard began to grow on my face. My hair lengthened, and darkened, but the glow remained and the little-boy stare. I saw I was Christ, but this must not be told. They had pinned me to the cross, with nothing but my eyes to tell them of my suffering. Behind me the cross grew taller, stronger, pine-sweet to the rough skin of my shoulder. Spring came, Eastertime, and palmleaves hung before my eyes, transparent green in the yellow sun, motionless in moonlight. They moved then, caressed by an unseen Hand. That it should have been me! I was ready to weep for it, such sweet relief, I let down a flood of great salt tears.

I splashed in a swoon, all groovy inside myself. "Ev-er-y-one is God!" sang the voice behind me. But to have freedom, and lovingness, all snug within, like sap in a green tree!

Back at the mirror I stood with genitals humbly in hand, and let myself waver into something soft and lovely, a woman, a beautiful lady, Cleopatra in fact on her barge, trailing for fish in the dusk where willows bent low to the water. Her dark face flushed brick as I gazed upon her in unflinching command. It was okay to be soft and alluring! I had a sensuous surface! And yet I was cruel! Like a cat I could spring and devour for mere pleasure of my prey. Nor did I know the slightest qualm: for the hot breath in my ear and dusky ass of her it was worth it. Dr. Tyrtan was just the opposite. "All these are masks of illusion," his voice intoned.

"That's what you think!"

The cruel mask of the queen was changing to a purplish pulp: the head of a prick, blood velvet to the touch, swollen ludicrously vulnerable yet at the same time lurching blindly to spit. Push it from me! Ah, much better—it stood upright now and satisfactory: staunch, athletic, intrepid, teleological. I decked it out in armor. A Japanese warrior stepped formal and menacing in his battle-dress. I let out my gutteral maniac cry and the warrior fell. A momentary horror—my own big brother, tortured, dying, crawling through the grass on the edge of a clearing, leaking blood from mouth and eyes and anus!

He had to be expiated—my idle life but a token. I fell on my sword.

"I die! By my own hand, true to promise. But I know now I will die and die again, only to be ceaselessly reborn!"

Nevertheless the mirror showed the little man in the waistcoat. His face was in shadow beneath his hat, and he did not budge.

Terrified I pulled backwards, jerking my head to the side. From the corner of my eye I saw the waistcoat melt into a winding-sheet. But the person inside was longer, his hairy blond legs stuck out below.

"I want that over with! Go! Go!" I whined. I tried to push my corpse away. There was no place else, no other space. It was either him or me.

"The wheel turns," said Dr. Tyrtan. "Let loose and float downstream."

With all my will I forced my arms down and opened my hands. The corpse then floated slowly out of sight. Without the Word, where would I be? I watched it till it vanished, a Viking now in horned helmet, ridiculous but comforting. At last I was getting hard again, stronger, tougher than ever. I wore swastikas on my shoulders and the brim of my hat! I could tell anyone to do anything—and I would! But who would tell me? I looked frantically for Dr. Tyrtan, who lay serenely on the sand.

The figure in the mirror shed his clothes like paper and stood revealed a court-jester in motley. "The joke's on me," I sobbed. "I'm not strong. I've been a clown my whole life, dancing with bells!" I wept copious maudlin tears. My whole cabinet wept with me. Our deep regrets, but the bombing must continue. Our weeping was readily drowned, however, by the screams of my mirror-image, who was now a bawling orphan baby.

I watched sadly as the baby screamed and flailed,

squirming in its own excrement. "You are innocent as a newborn babe," drawled the voice of Dr. Tyrtan.

In a childlike singsong I repeated, "Innocent . . . new-born . . ."

I stared into the mirror, nose pressed flat against the glass like that of my boyhood father when he stared into the candy-shop. But oh such candy as we have now! I watched while my breath steamed a fragile circle. Slowly, very slowly, the form of the babe began to change. "Holy, Holy," I murmured. "Holy Babe . . ."

I watched in empty fixation, slack-mouthed and dribbling, as the baby's shape melted to a formless mass, as its nameless segments drifted apart, came into smaller pieces, and began to recombine. Gradually another shape appeared, but what was it? The thing was fixed and final, parts clearly etched in hard black edges, but it made no sense as a whole. And the matter was of no little import. I had to stay and see it through; I could not be born again without some vision of my essential insides. Wasn't that what they'd said? To see myself!

Yea verily, the mass quivered and began to rotate, turned upside down, rippled, settled, and I saw . . . then . . . horror! *The head of the deer, bright blood spurting from its severed neck!*

Wee Alex screamed, fell headlong into blackness.

Beyond the curtain rich music played. The Resurrection Cantata: I knew it—at last, an old known thing. In my submarine I gently rose through warm deep waters. The recognition comforted me, yet I could not stop sobbing. If only I could nose on and on and never come up for air! For I had seen my own desire, known myself killer as well as deer.

No choice but to rise from heavy depths that pushed me upward. I surfaced and lay sobbing in the center of the room, my head in Tyrtan's lap. Through wet lashes I saw the room itself returned to normal proportions, fire and mirror calmly sunk to their usual state. Dr. Tyrtan half-reclined on silk-covered pillows as he stroked my hair.

". . . beautiful, beautiful, a pure, unfettered soul. What you've suffered comes only from your openness. I've never given the Drug to anyone as wide open. . . ."

I was choking still. The purity business was wrong, ridiculous, stupid. I should have fled from the easiness, but where could I flee to? I was in too deeply, and only this man could help me out. If one could only know a little more! Then one could care for oneself, one could bear it.

"Where does the blackness come from?" I finally asked through numbed lips. "The blackness that always comes?"

"From your imagination only. The blackness is unreal. Only the Clear Light is real."

"But where does death come from? And violence, the lust to kill? And ugliness and pain and suffering?"

He calmly stroked my hair.

"I wish I could tell you how beautiful you are. . . ."

I submitted to this, though it galled me. I had to wait—and then I might be told! I had no strength yet to demand.

But the doctor was still calming me and flattering. If he could get that over with! It made things worse. I knew I'd never crack—I just wanted to know.

I sat up and smiled to show the man I was okay.

"You lay it on a bit thick." I watched Tyrtan anxiously—so important he not misunderstand!

All he said was, "Yes?"

"It's not necessary," I said. "I'm all right. In fact I have some things to tell you. From now on messages will come through me as well. We must listen to one another. And now I have these words for you. You needn't try so hard. You needn't take all that good care of me. You needn't make sure of me. You couldn't anyway. It isn't necessary. I'm arriving on schedule, all on my own."

He looked at me humorously from pale shining eyes. He shrugged his shoulders, let out a pouf of laughter. He sighed. "I've received so much abuse . . ." he said, pondering his outstretched knees.

"Of course you have," I said. "And you are reacting just as you, being you, would react. All is as it should be. But in the future you won't come on so hard. The last thing you want is for people to see your defensiveness."

"Am I defensive, Alex?" he asked with a sudden grin. "Have I kept anything from you?"

"Not exactly." All at once I was confused. Perhaps I'd gone too far. So hard to keep hold of my thoughts, such as they were! "Not exactly," I said again. "So many things I want to know . . . but . . . I suppose it can't be forced. Knowing . . . it isn't just a matter of knowing. I can't say it right—these words have less meaning. . . ."

The redhaired man smiled fondly, kindly upon me. What in the world did I expect? Here, after all, was attention, love, patience. Things would come. I couldn't even remember what I'd been thinking of. My thoughts were mesmerized by the man in front of me who'd been attending so kindly and lovingly all night long as a novice thrashed in the arrogance of his first real visions. The man had waited and watched without scorn, without laughter. I was overwhelmed with awe of him.

"I must be so much trouble for you!"

"Trouble?"

"Maybe you don't see it," I said, "but I feel so . . . presumptuous. It occurs to me that hundreds of others go through the same thing. Or do they?"

He nodded, smiling.

"They all come to you, don't they? They think no one else will do. They think it's just the two of you. You have to re-live their whole lives with them. Every damn one must think he's God and expect you to bow down to him!"

He sighed, his head flopped on his shoulder.

"Once I was merely a medicine man, Alex. I had a taste then of the terrific responsibility of letting people come to you. But I was shielded by the game-device of the professional attitude. My patients risked everything, while I gave nothing and asked nothing—except money. But from the first instant of my first ecstasy, I knew there are no limits to what a man can bear. You ask what pain is? Pain comes from artificial limits. Whereas infinite acceptance can yield only bliss. And now a greater burden has been laid upon me. I must carry on my shoulders the cast-off vanities of thousands."

"You must be very weary," I said tenderly.

I knew I had been right to trust this man. He was part of the unity that had guided my whole life. The one you finally had to trust was the one you could trust, should trust, were meant to trust.

I could see that Dr. Tyrtan knew this too. For Dr. Tyrtan trusted me. We gazed fondly at one another, almost like lovers—

A grating rasp—the sliding oaken door was violently shoved open!

I leapt up in terror at the violation.

"NO!" I shouted.

Seymour entered with head held menacingly low, feet planted far apart, apelike, vicious, stoned out of his skull. He had moved the door as a man might cast aside a screen. His heavy body was compact and massive, transformed by an appalling power.

I shrank as Dr. Tyrtan glided to Seymour's side. The walls of the room were waving before my eyes like so many strips of rubber, squeezing me in toward the hateful red-eyed animal who stood glaring as Dr. Tyrtan held his arm and whispered in his ear.

Suavely Dr. Tyrtan whispered, but Seymour was growling ominously, even barking. His gorilla body was jumping to stomp and smash the former friend who had stolen his place. For myself I was utterly afraid that the life would be crushed out of me: a deep desperate panic cleaved from throat to bowels.

I edged toward the open door. Without taking his eyes from Seymour, Dr. Tyrtan checked me.

"No Alex, no—we had better not leave this room."

Seymour laughed brutally. "He gave you a double dose—four times what he took himself! You'll be high for days! You'll do anything he wants!"

Dr. Tyrtan tightened his grip on Seymour's arm. Seymour looked stupidly at the hand squeezing him, and his sneer collapsed in blubbery softness. The pink had drained from Tyrtan's face; his popping eyes were fixed in absolute command. Fat tears rolled down Seymour's cheeks.

"I'm sorry," he whimpered.

Too late! I bolted on out of there!

I went running stumbling sailing bouncing. Through psychotic corridors, door after door opening one upon another, eyes staring, mouth gaping, bodies billowing and reaching out as I twisted to get by. The empty one-beat bass throbbed on in the spaceless hollow track of corridors. I ran into a bathroom where shiny tiles reflected horrible melting burning faces. Bland heads floated in behind me and ballooned calmly to the side as I ran out. The wooden walls held shadowed prisoners in their dull gloss, the moldings crawled with prickly insects and writhing wet-bellied snakes.

Somewhere behind me Dr. Tyrtan drifted in pursuit, face puckered and troubled; but he too was stumbling, forcing himself along through sheer experience against the shapeless proliferation of the house.

At last he cornered me in the cubic room with six mirrored surfaces. As Tyrtan reached I squirmed, and we bounced from wall to wall like frenzied bats or astronauts in a capsule. Limbs parted and floated bye-bye, reduplicated as they cleaved through planes of doubletake, slow-motion, as in the mirror maze of a fun house, where exits are long since sealed and earthly space a dustpocket trapped in endless recess of reflection. We swam through a collection of cornerless envelopes, sealed off by crossing shards of light, fragmented in spaceless timeless re-refractions. Wide-eyed and open-mouthed we sailed in anti-particles of mirror light, our hands and feet yearning for the touch of matter. Music was heard—the weird slow tones of outer space—as we flew in our lost ballet.

My eyes were closed and face slack. I lay stretched out where I had at last been brought to rest—in the corridor outside the mirror room.

My feet began a mild kicking. A tension fluttered up through trunk and shoulders to my upstretched arms, to my hands—which were holding for dear life to Dr. Tyrtan's ankles.

Tyrtan, standing, had got hold of his book. He heaved and sucked himself together, and began to read aloud.

"If thou canst not maintain the bliss of illumination, Remember:

The hallucinations, the divine visions
Will tear the veil from thine eyes, will teach thee all.
Recall the unity of all things, the ecstasy of the Clear
 Light.
Let it guide thee to thy new life, thy true self.
In confusion, remember the heroes who have trod this
 path before thee,
And above all, trust to the power of thy guide."

He looked down, amused I'm sure. I'd laid my cheek against his slippered foot.

"Beyond the vain frenzy of life is Ultimate Reality—
The Void.
 [An echo boomed: *The Void*]
Accept the voidness of thine own mind as Buddhahood.
Embrace it and dissolve thyself in the spirit of the
 Buddha."

The serious rose-flushed face of him bloomed in my vision. An effulgence appeared in the air, swam down Tyrtan's head, materialized into a cleric's collar round his neck. Ah, then! Then at last, for one moment, I could look to my heart's content at the seeking driven young man who had stopped for a photograph just one generation before, at the outset of his journey to a new land and a new life, to serve a Master who dwelt in the halls of eternal grace.

I was on my knees, embracing Tyrtan's waist with all my might, holding on. . . .

13

HALF-STEERING, HALF-SUPPORTING, Dr. Tyrtan helped me through the halls, which had diminished to a pale solidity in the first light of dawn.

"Don't try to talk," he said. "It was all my fault. You must beware of hangups now."

He was taking me back to the meditation room.

"Is he coming back?" I said.

"No. Absolutely not."

"I don't want him to come back."

Dr. Tyrtan giggled. "He wouldn't hurt you. That's only a game you play."

I stretched on a lumpy mattress, propping my head to keep on guard.

"I'm afraid of so many things," I confessed.

"Be afraid then! Sink to the bottom and let fear do its worst!"

Little bolts of terror shot up my nerves from time to time. But there was no bottom; I simply could not imagine walking down the street. I wanted to reach for Dr. T's ankle and hold onto it. I held out my hand but made no contact. It was too much the same.

"You're playing a no-win game," he told me. "You want to be comforted, but to get that comfort you have to regress into a frightened little boy."

"You're right," I said, when I thought about it. "But I don't know how to change."

"You've been lying here poring over your fears. Well pore over them some more. Take all the time you like. Whenever you get bored there's always the rest."

"What rest?"

"Life."

"But life is an illusion!"

Dr. Tyrtan shook his head and put on another record. Immediately a man in a top hat striped pants and spats came walking along. He brushed back his tails his processed hair and spread his hands across the keyboard. He feathered for a while, taking it easy. But in no time flat he'd build a syncopated thickness. And even then, he built up more, more than could be imagined, that scheming scheming fond foolish kindly old man. He went romping up a cloud of blues, steaming with all his might.

Well okay, merely incredible. But then a shower of octaves; below, a walking bass—and a third hand appeared, jamming the middle with impossible chord progressions!

I didn't believe it—felt my shoulders tremble. While the old man went on to carry it out past the edge of time.

"The life-flow is not an illusion," said Dr. Tyrtan.

"Be quiet!"

I was listening to the ancient father as he sang in a rending thinness of most delicate love, gently feathering and tinkling his honest song along. I thought of all the tinklings over the years, the finger by finger work of it. So that smoothness can be smooth and funky funky, the lifting of each pinky without hesitation. Why bother, as we know so well? But why not? The sheer will of it, to go ahead, through years of neglect and drowned-out supper music, ten hours a night and sleep on the bus with your bottle and bad memories. But you could see it there, that will, that senseless pride, beyond his gold-toothed blubbered smile, the drops of sweat each one a grain of time as the outer life outdone goes on anyway and here it is and the hell with it! Because the man came through, he spoke truly, he made it all worthwhile, for a while.

It could be done—if you had the will. And if it turned out that way.

Did I please you? asked the sweating charming tinkle tinkle. (Knowing secretly it had laid us waste and gone on by.)

Yes, my man. God bless you. Life-flow no illusion. Only people were illusions. And me with no sounding-board to keep them from me. Or to sound my sound. Whatever would I do, later, with me? Best not to think about it, drop back to stupidity. *Profound* stupidity, man, the profounder the better. I managed, and toward the end I sailed into a calm at the still heart of the last long sweet piano.

Faint grey dawn-light showed in the high slitted windows. I lay quietly. The Drug was wearing off. All the time it was wearing off, but it came back in surges. I lay quiet and wary, beginning to slip back again to my old habit of comparing.

I looked once more at my companion, who sat stony, trunk rigid, eyes fixed on the far wall, face bleak and unsmiling. Rusty stubble flecked his face unevenly. Faint lines creased the joining of neck and jaw, and beyond one corner of the mouth a muscle pouch twitched.

"You look older in daylight," I said.

He started. Where had he been? His eyes were streaked like soft rock.

"I'm what you call tired," he said slowly. "In my

medical days I would have prescribed myself a long rest. But now I like to play with these concepts of illness. . . ."

"I don't follow," I yawned, "when you talk about concepts."

"You know, you have a very good mind, Alex—"

He flashed out almost bitterly and broke off as quickly as he had begun. All at once he was lost in reverie.

"My own mind was never so good. Always stupid in school, bad grades and so on. Even as a doctor I never quite measured up. Some of them thought well of me, but they didn't know, not really. When I did research I always had to fake my statistics. . . ."

He turned his wicked smile on me, warning warning. Make of this what you will, but be careful.

What the hell, I had a devilish smile of my own.

"You mean even when you taught at med school you falsified experiments?"

"I wouldn't put it that way. Your categories of truth and falsehood hold only within a certain basket of rules. And I plunged through the bottom of the basket when I came to the Drug. For a while I resisted—played careful young scientist testing dangerous drug etcetera. But how do you even begin, say, to set up a control group, when you're either in this world or another one? Who's controlling who? Where is the observer standing? I got beyond that. Otherwise I'd have gotten nowhere. And of course I've found a whole generation that knew right away what I was groping for.

"But the problem at first was to come up with something to convince your so-called scientists. They think I'm a quack, a faith-healer . . . but then again, I was just telling you that in *their* terms I was *always* mediocre."

He bore down again with his sea slate eyes.

"Am I mediocre, Alex?"

I had to laugh. "Not as long as you have the Drug!"

Tyrtan hesitated, but I kept on grinning. So he grinned too and gave out his weird cackle.

I cackled too till something gave way inside. Something physical, a bone in my chest perhaps. A general softening? Some of my bones had gone floppy and rotten.

"Why do you smile?" asked Dr. Tyrtan.

"I don't know. I don't know."

I was shaking my head from side to side, trying to joggle the switch back on. Sudden tears streamed down my face. The Drug was working despite all I could do. I could not blot a soft clinging feeling, like the melting center of a chocolate caramel. I was affected by Tyrtan's tiredness, his fragile bravery, his mediocrity. I wept softly, as a young girl weeps.

"I guess I just . . . feel sorry. No. No. When I think of how . . . alone . . . you are . . . I feel such . . . tenderness."

I was glad of my tenderness; the Drug had shown how good it was to be tender.

Dr. Tyrtan spoke deliberately from very near.

"You *feel* tenderness—as a *thought*? What about tenderness *like this*!"

He leaned close and brought his long soft hands along my face. He stroked me.

The music had stopped. I looked at him very hard.

"Oh," I said. "You want me to be your baby."

I got up and walked out of the house.

Fibers of perfume clung in the faint silver air. The new morning was abnormally warm, with rich clouds swelling in turbulence. Over in the East a slit of pale bright light opened and closed among the churning clouds. I stopped on the front lawn to piss in a flower bed, in fascination at my urine sparkling in a rainbow to tunnel radiant beneath the snow's thin crust. As my stream declined the warm wind whipped it up into blazing droplets which took no color from the dankness of the atmosphere.

A thrill of freedom raced recoupling through my veins. The long night was over, and I was outdoors, alive, free forever of that suffocating house. I had taken the Drug and come through.

From the corner of my eye I had an impression of a great penis snaking and thrashing off beyond the black cloudbanks. Ah ha, I thought, the wrathful God, with his swollen crooked head! I strode off jingling up the hill to get a better look—and saw a bolt of lightning flash silent in the western blackness. I breathed deep, filled my lungs with electric ozone.

Dr. Tyrtan caught up with me on the rocky uphill path and trailed along in controlled supplication.

"I can't stop you," he said, "but you ought not to leave, Alex. I must assume reponsibility. If you're upset it's my fault, Alex. You aren't ready yet to put things in perspective. I wish you'd come back to the house for a good long sleep. Then we can talk things over to your heart's content."

I plunged uphill through the woods where charm-dolls dangled. At the top of the ridge I turned and saw the huge house sprawled below like a grim medieval castle in the grey dawnlight. Dr. Tyrtan scrambled up and took my elbow.

"Relax," I said.

"You, too."

We half-looked at each other and averted our faces.

"How 'bout a walk?" I said.

We walked along the ridge where the thick breeze pushed through our clothes and swathed our limbs in air. I stopped and leaned against the wall to watch the far-off storm seep blackly up into the sky. Beyond the wall the canyon fell off steeply into a gulf where daylight had not yet penetrated.

I was getting jumpy again with too many thoughts in my head. I could sense Dr. Tyrtan at my side peering at me too damn attentively.

"You're beginning to come down now, Alex. You must think what kind of re-entry you want to make."

"Yes, yes," I said. "I can't decide between a swinging vine from the Eiffel Tower or a basket among the bullrushes."

Tyrtan laughed, more or less.

"Seriously," he said, "for your own good. I'd be a poor guide if I didn't warn you you're going to have problems picking up your old life. You'll find your customary ego won't fit you anymore. I wonder what you'll do? Perhaps your 'mind' will reassert itself—try to repress what you've seen tonight. That might be convenient."

"Gee, convenience!—that would be quite a change! Can you promise that? I'll just take it easy, huh, from now on?"

"Sure," said Tyrtan, "like you're taking it easy right now."

I had to admit I was getting tense. I couldn't laugh with him any better than he could with me.

"Never underestimate," he warned, "the power of society. In Chicago I gave the Drug to a woman whose little girl had been kidnapped on the dunes. Naturally the medical doctors had only reinforced her hysteria. She was playing the distraught mother game, you dig? She had terrible torments at first on the Drug. She had to relive all the bad conscience of motherhood. All the hatred she had felt for the child, the desire to punish, smother, and so forth, was churning up in her cells. She tortured herself for hours. But finally she let go—and her ability to love came back, not fixated merely to one child, but spreading freely to the whole creation.

"Once I'd opened her, she realized that the appearance or disappearance of her child was simply part of the shimmer of living energy, an expression of the one supreme Self which plays an eternal hide and seek, dismembering itself as the many and remembering itself as the One. She wouldn't have to put it that way—but she was way beyond the need for words.

"Now if only she'd made a decent re-entry, that woman would have been reborn. But she got nervous. She couldn't face her husband. She knew that once she dropped the hysteria he'd blame her for losing the child. So as she came down from her trip she got hung up on the visceral *chakra,* where images of the bowels and early toilet-training manifest themselves. And therefore she reimprinted an image of herself as a bad, guilty person. At that time we didn't know as many techniques to guide a person past that point.

"When she got home, her only solution was to dig herself deeper. She became catatonic. Her husband played his part by calling back the authorities and having her institutionalized—dig the word? They left her only one way out—to hate the person who had given her the Drug.

"And the result was another slander," he concluded grimly.

"Did they ever find the child?" I asked.

Tyrtan didn't hear the question. He was staring at his feet as we picked our way along the ridge, climbing higher.

"Did they find the child?" I repeated.

"What?—I don't think so. I really don't know."

Down by the house the trees were roiling. The sky churned higher as the black edge of the storm drew near.

"You're saying I don't have to be like that?"

Dr. Tyrtan was blank.

"I don't have to be like that woman?"

"No. Yes! You can choose to re-enter any way you like. Only remember: not everyone will understand what you've been through. Don't try to force it; they'll only lock you up. Just dance your worldly dance, do what's expected of you. Get what you can."

"But suppose I get tired of contemplating the Void? Even if it's there!

"I mean," I added, "I'm not sure I wouldn't get more kicks from my own little ego-pleasures—"

"Alex, you worry me when you talk like that. You're your own worst enemy."

Despite myself I giggled. "Oh I know, I know. But . . . well . . . what do you do for sex, for example?"

"What are you driving at?"

"Well, there could hardly be anything more petty and games-playing."

"Games-playing, yes, in terms of your Western aggressive genital sex! That was one of the first things we up-leveled. We now know that the two-person set can yield the most exquisite pleasures, journeys deep into the realm of pure sensation—"

"But *how*?"

He set his jaw. "There is something," he said slowly, "called Tantric Sex, an ancient Eastern lore, which when practiced by those deeply skilled in its ways can yield a total orgasmic firing of every cell in your body, from your toenails to your eyelids."

"I'm ready," I said. "But I notice you talk about skills. I thought we all had the same skills?"

"Alex, if I were a Zen master I'd slap you now. Your mind makes contradictions where nature knows none."

"Then tell me more about this Tantric Sex. Maybe that will be it for me. Could you have it with an eighty-year-old woman?"

He grimaced.

"Theoretically. But it's pure disaster in the hands of the uninitiated."

"A *very ugly* eighty-year-old woman?"

Now Tyrtan was walking ahead of me, walking faster and faster.

"Alex, I'm beginning to be disappointed with you. You're making re-entry very difficult for yourself. I advise you to stop talking. You can't penetrate the Eternal Mysteries by asking schoolboy questions. If you're serious in your commitment you'll spend the rest of your life in discipline and meditation. Don't try to learn everything at once; there'll be many more sessions for you, thousands of fresh imprintations. . . ."

"But suppose I'm not serious? Suppose I just want to have fun?"

Dr. Tyrtan didn't answer. We were climbing higher and higher as the blackness rose up in the West, pushing grey clouds before it like dirty slush.

"And besides," I shouted against the wind, "I still don't understand! If it's all an illusion, why am I still me? What are we doing here?"

He wheeled around and faced me. I thought for a second he would hit me in the belly. My nerves rang like firebells.

"To answer that I'd have to go into the whole evolution of the so-called civilized mind. But why make problems for yourself?"

I wanted to turn and run down. To knock Tyrtan

over and run up. Instead I closed my eyes and made another problem.

"Suppose that little girl were tortured—"

"You don't know that!"

"But she might have been! That's the whole point! It happens every day! Don't you read the war news!"

He tried to turn but I grabbed him by the arm. He looked down sneeringly at my hand but I held him fast. I could feel him shivering through his silk suitcoat.

"Suppose I didn't?" he said. "Suppose I didn't read your beloved war news?"

"Suppose they didn't just kill her?" I said. "So she could simply split out to mingle with the Clear Light. Suppose they cut her up, made her die real slow? If so . . . was her pain real?"

"What do you think?" he sneered.

I grabbed his collar and shook him violently.

"Answer me! *Was her pain real*?"

He twisted convulsively and shook loose of me. "I'm not afraid of you, Alex!"

I stood holding myself, quivering as fear and anger swept me in wave after wave.

Meanwhile Dr. Tyrtan had got hold of himself in another way.

"Frightened people do frightened things," he said, "precisely because they have not seen the Light."

"But are people real?" I continued. My voice was strange and dangerous, as if it came from some even angrier person caught inside me. "Is pain real?" that person asked again.

Dr. Tyrtan had nothing more to say. He looked upon me with deep compassion. But the man inside had no damn use for his compassion. He'd wanted an Answer and he'd gotten one. The Answer was zero. And the man inside was far from over the Drug. However I leaned, he was in there shoving.

We'd got to the peak of the ridge. There was enough light now to see a long way down the steep sides of the canyon. I could feel us getting very tiny as the sky uncoiled above and the trees whipped and rolled below and the warm wind sucked hungrily at our meager flesh.

But I found I could shoot beams of light from my diamond eyes. It came to me to jump back in and go all the way. I began to shout out against the wind, not caring whoever heard me.

"It's a world of dew!" I shouted. "Zero! Zero! Olley Olley Ox-en, All in Free-ee! Free at last, Hon-est-lee-ee! I'm all in free, do what I please, because *nothing matters*! NOTHING MATTERS!"

My soul beat heavy wings and lifted me soaring up onto the retaining wall.

"Ah ha! I could jump! Look at me! I could jump now! I hear it calling, calling, my whole life long! And now I could go! It's up to me!"

I raced along the top of the wall, leaping crazily, my thick hair streaming past my ears like a winged helmet. I wheeled in glory to look down on my earthbound companion.

The poor man stood with hands on hips, frowning, so I sang him "Dear, dear, what can the matter be?"

"Get down, Alex."

"Are you telling me what to doooo?" I slyly keened.

"You can do whatever you want. I trust you Alex."

"Why I want to fly. Like a teatray in the sky!"

He had to follow me from below as I strode along in magic certainty of footing. I remember stopping and opening my arms to the seething heavens. Let them take me then, now, while I accepted the whole of it, and could not be diminished.

"No one ever does anything high he wouldn't do normally," recited Tyrtan behind me.

"But you're forgetting!" I shouted. "Shame on you! No such thing as normal! I can do as I please. I'm upleveled forever! The Answer Drug has given me The Answer!"

I wasn't playing games anymore—I was set to go beyond the game world, once and for all! It was my fate to take to the ultimate everything Tyrtan had taught me. I had the power now and I wasn't afraid to use it. Oh no! Because I knew full well that to be afraid at all was to be totally in fear.

"Alex, listen to me! As long as you are in the game sphere, you must take responsibility!"

"Think about *responsibility*!"

"And you think what happens if you kill yourself! The authorities would come—there'd be an investigation. Our whole movement would be misunderstood and suppressed!"

Too much! I capered divinely as lightning cracked beyond and the canyon yawned below.

"That's all an illusion," I crooned. "Don't you get the message? Don't you recollect? Nothing matters! Why, you're the guide! You mixed the elixir, one shilling a box! Be off, or I'll kick you downstairs!"

A blast of wind caught me teetering and I nearly fell. The pale man shrank wincing.

"*The Void!*" I sang him. "Think of the Void! Who cares about authorities! Or understanding! Oh holy birdshit—understanding!

"I don't care—only mortals care! You poor silly guru! That's why I was sent here! I'll show you—in just one second!"

I arched my back in a lovely longbow, belly toward Tyrtan, arms out behind, neck flopped on high, goodbye

—and I dropped from the wall. But just for fun I caught the edge with my hands and hung there, foot-paddling in the gulf.

Tyrtan threw himself forward and grabbed my wrists. So I let go, and the shock of my weight tugged us over and down. Tyrtan braced, holding on for dear life—his, not mine. I was laughing up at him in pure fearless glee!

"God Damn you!" he said.

I spat in his face.

He was weeping now as he clung to my wrists. I went limp, made not the slightest effort to climb back up. And he lacked the strength to pull me. "Let go!" I shouted, but my voice was drowned in thunder.

Looking up through his chalky eyeballs I could read his single panicked thought: that letting go would mean the law. Typical bourgeois hangup. The pit beyond and the black wall of sky were the looming of a mammoth cop—and the lightning flash the crackle of Big Daddy's razorstrop. His powder lips were praying for the Judge to come and get it over with!

Suddenly I swung myself up like the devil's own acrobat. The lurch sickened Tyrtan, he nearly fainted with dread. Before he could recover I had hold of him and dragged him up entirely onto the wall.

I pulled his face right up against mine.

"So you want responsibility," I said. "Be responsible for my death!"

I plunged and he clutched me back. But I wouldn't have cared if he hadn't. For a minute we grappled on the loose stones, as I laughed and gasped for air. He was tickling me again—his wrestling tickled! I grabbed him and held him out over the edge.

"Twinkle twinkle little breath. Could it be you're scared of death?"

I threw him like a dried leaf back down to the ground.

I stood alone on the wall, watching a sheet of rain sweep toward me, free to decide yes or no.

Tyrtan had crawled off. He half-lay on his elbows, head drooping, unable to look.

"You won't jump, Alex. I know you won't."

"Look at me," I commanded. Thunder boomed up from the canyon, enveloping us, shaking the earth. A stone fell loose from the wall and plummeted. But I kept my balance, waiting, and Tyrtan was forced to look up and meet my eye.

I raised my arms again and offered silent blessing to the whole senseless scene. Lightning, thunder. It was quite some show.

I could have jumped boat if I wanted to. It would have been relaxing to cleave freely through the air. I fancied I would blast myself a monumental hole.

But that was boring. Of all the odd things! I was bored! A laugh on me again, and not a special new one either, but the oldest laugh in the world. Yet it was laughable as ever! I floated lightly to the path, where I lay in hysterical hilarity, pounding the ground with my fists.

14

THE STORM CLOSED SWIFTLY over our heads, a crack of lightning bleached the air, and rain swept down in torrents.

I lay wallowing like a jolly hog in rain and mud. Whatever was Tyrtan shouting as he tugged at my arm? I lifted my chinny-chin-chin and snorted the man away.

"What do you know?" I squealed. "I'm going to live!"

I jumped to my feet and went galloping down the long hill, in and out among the snapping crying trees, twisting and leaping in a frenzy.

When I reached the backyard I collapsed face down where the snow had melted into the slick grass. The rain had slackened and I could soon feel Tyrtan's whisper in my ear. But why should I care, I'd found completeness. Soothing luncheon music as I slime away in the cool wet green. . . .

At last Tyrtan got me to a covered bower. I found a wooden plaque with a painted Buddha which I pulled down and sat upon. A little speaker piped feeble pentatones: I wrenched it loose from its wires.

Then I pulled inside myself and sat shivering as the rain battered on our roof of vines and planks and withered leaves and leaked down spattering my trembling shoulders. I was jangled again; couldn't look at Tyrtan's face. I wanted never again to look at it.

"You'll catch a chill," he said, lightly laying his arm across my back.

"Don't touch me!" I cornily cried.

He jumped up. I flinched. Both of us were in a fine state of postflight jitters.

"I want to go home." Now I looked up. "Drive me home."

"You said you would stay!" he blurted. "That's part of our contract!" He gestured wildly and both of us shrank. "You have to come in the house and sleep. I told you that before. You're trying to back out on me!"

"I don't owe you anything."

He sat down to get himself together. Neither of us spoke as the rain slackened again and then spilled heavily down once more.

"Why don't you trust your feelings?" he asked. "Remember?"

"Because I feel *the need* inside me. And it's in you too!"

He frowned, he shrugged. "You know I can't keep you against your will. But it's my duty to talk it over. Just what's driving you, Alex? What are you running from?"

I sat trembling and wondering where my strength had gone to. Had I already lost the freedom of the wall? And the triumph! What triumph?

I was clearly fearing now, whereas Tyrtan's voice had steadied. He repeated his question. And how could I answer? I sat frozen in suspicion. I knew he was thinking of going to the house for help. He would get his big Quentin. But he knew if I bolted I would get off the estate before they could catch me. And then I might babble. Or so he thought. It would never do.

"Where are you, Alex?" he cautiously inquired.

"Thinking. Really thinking."

"Yes?"

"Yes."

"What about?"

"About why you've got to drive me back to the city. Or lend me keys to a car."

"And why is that?"

"My roommate Benjy. I see him standing in the bathroom, all in white. I send him away, but he keeps coming back."

I looked at him as deadly as I could. The rain splattered on the leaves like drippings from a faucet.

"I can't take you," he said slowly. "There's no car available."

He may have had keys right in his pocket. What if I tried to take them? He deserved it for lying. But I was too shaken—could think only of killing or being killed.

"If you don't trust me," he said evenly, "I can press this buzzer and summon others who do."

I knew the buzzer was disconnected, but still it frightened me.

"You have a lot of power," I said sadly.

"Power is the ultimate turn-on," he said. "That's one of the things we'll discuss, as soon as you're ready."

"Never be ready," I murmured.

"You're no judge of that!" he snapped. "Your values are way off, Alex. You think for instance you can drive a car. Well let me tell you, if you thought you were scared before, at any time of your journey, you'll really learn what fear is, once you get in an automobile with the Drug still pushing. And of course I'd be driving, not you. You'd have no control whatever. You don't realize how high you still are. Look, look here!"

I did not turn my head but allowed Tyrtan to put his

hand on my neck and turn it for me. In a hanging bronze shield I saw the face of a young, sad boy with cavernous pupils. Pathetically young! And yet there was determination—he was nobody's boy but his own.

Was that Tyrtan in the mirror, arms high to hit me on the head!

I spun around. He snickered a high toothy whinny.

"Let me hold the wheel and you'll be terrified, Alex! Because I don't think you trust me anymore. If you did you wouldn't run from me."

Silence.

"Do you trust me, Alex? Do you want to talk sensibly, calmly?"

I nodded.

"Shall we go inside now, like good friends, take a long nap and see what we shall see?"

No journey was over, he continued, until the traveler slowly retraced his steps. To jump sideways from the path was fatal. I would come into the warmth, rub dry before a fire, change clothes, get nourishing soup inside me, sleep fast in a warm dry bed. Tomorrow I would meditate and sleep. Dr. Tyrtan had his hand on my shoulder again, bearing down with his depthless eyes. The hand tightened, as it had with Seymour. . . .

Slowly, with difficulty, I grasped the hand and put it off me. I turned my back and walked out into the rain. Then panic poured through me and I started to run. Tyrtan was hot behind me, screaming for help at the top of his lungs.

Sure enough, a heavy figure lurched angrily from the porch, lunged through the rain and tackled not myself but Dr. Tyrtan! Seymour the Serene had made no mistake. He held his master madly in his arms, hissing "Let him go! Let him go!"

I ran into the house, thinking to grab Benjy's motorcycle key from the pocket of my coat which lay on a mattress in the meditation room. Except that it didn't: the room was bare and dull, yielding nothing to my frantic search among the trinkets and trappings.

The door slammed shut with a crash. Seymour again! I put up my fists. But he went right past, grabbed up Tyrtan's heavy book, and threw it into the middle of the long mirror! The whole thing dissolved, like ice falling off a roof.

"Nice shot!" said I, and he held out his hand to be slapped.

My old friend Seymour grabbed a long window-hook, pulled down the mandala from the ceiling and tore it to shreds between his teeth. For love betrayed he kicked the burnt logs and ashes from the fireplace and sprinkled them about the room. Meanwhile I had turned on the phonograph and a Bach aria crept out into the ashy air, a jazzed-up version not quite on speed and twisted badly out of shape. With the music sagging lagging thumping wailing, I managed to jerk out a number of tiles, which Seymour scaled through the little stained windows. With fire tongs he demolished a tape recorder and used the wiring to decapitate the plaster Buddhas and strangle the plastic ones. He got a fire going in the middle of the room, and stoked it with wooden idols and incense burners. I shredded the tapestries and threw them on, causing a choking smoke to rise. It was wonderful how things fell apart at our touch, as if made of dust. If only we'd had a blowtorch we'd have welded them together in one massive obscenity. With shards of glass Seymour carved the mattresses and prayer rugs. At times he fell, cutting himself on the broken glass, till his body was caked with mud and blood and ashes.

The music seemed to pull our minds with rubber bands. Seymour got down from the wall a double-bladed feudal hacking ax, used in days of chivalry to lop arms and legs from presumptuous parapet-climbers. As I flattened out against the wall he lay about him pulverizing the mantelpiece, woodwork, fixtures, hacking every protrusion to a fine rubble which he kicked into his blupping fire in the middle of the room.

Soon the fire was out of control. Flames licked at the crawly ceiling as I cowered and suety Seymour danced a heathen dance around the flames. Dance of the absurd abyss, he called it. The holy mind-stomp. Dedicated to the one true Master, whoever he may be. Oh Buddha, I chanted to the rubber Bach, bless me in thy sparkling subtle dazzling radiance, and let the rainbow blood of the life-force flow up and down my entrails, till truly I am one with the pulsing sun, and orgasmic fire glows in every cell. Blessed art thou among women, and blessed is the drug of thy womb Soma.

Then to my horror Seymour picked up his ax again and chopped wildly at the column which held up the outer corner of the room. I unlocked the door and rushed out. Quentin, Jacky and others flew by the other way to put out the fire. The population had been wakened and churned mildly up and down the halls in their nightgowns.

I stood on the covered porch, uncertain. Ghostly figures flew this way and that. I wanted badly to go out and climb a tree. Tyrtan ran right by without seeing me, but still I was scared. I'd started for the driveway, when someone called my name. It was Amber, back on the porch, clinging to one of the wooden supports. She was disheveled, haggard, looking years older—and imploring me, for what I do not know, not to this day, though I think of it often. A little cry flew from her lips like a rising shade. Then Quentin had her by the waist and began to stroke her flanks as one calms an animal.

Whomp! A great dull thud as from the inside Seymour plopped his bulk against the pillar. Once, twice, and a corner of the house caved in, the roof buckled—and sagged halfway to the ground in an *oof* of steaming dust.

I bolted for a station wagon in the side drive. Tugged at the door—locked! Slipped, fell in the mud, rain pelting down, got up somehow and tried the other door. It opened—and there were keys in the ignition! But Tyrtan was coming after! I saw him dash from the house!

I downed the accelerator and the car lurched backwards. Tyrtan had jumped in one of the limousines. The lawn rubbed up and down against my face like a green crepe towel. And in my ears the fine jabbing needles of Amber's weeping.

My car swerved hysterically across the lawn and through some flower beds, digging ruts and flattening shrubbery. I spun along the edge of the woods, trying to hide among the trees, and smashed head-on into the wooden tower.

The tower wobbled like a windblown lily. Mona Sweetan stuck her little head out completely stoned, cackling gleefully as she waved on the wand of the storm.

Struggling with my own poor shoulders against the elements, the car, the Drug, I managed to back away from the tower and head out the driveway. With careful aim I split the center of the bridge and plunged down the long green tunnel. As I passed beneath the stone entranceway I saw Tyrtan's limousine in the rearview mirror heading right into my forehead. Baffled for a moment, I could not choose the proper plane upon which to flee. Luckily the gate was open; I spun the wheel; my car jerked off the heavenly property and onto the dirt road.

Behind me the sleek cruiser took his turn too fast,

skidded and nearly went into a ditch, righted himself and came on like black gas.

On the porch I had seen the heavenly community lining up to peer out after us in solemn zombie reverence. As I drove their faces faded slowly, only their eyes remaining, as our cars streaked down the road to the squeak of far-off sobbing and the muffled crash of the passing storm.

Rained when I found you rained when I left and on through the rain I roared, russian-rouletting the red lights on half a chance Tyrtan would draw the kicker. Meanwhile his face unfolded like a black rose till it filled mirror and windshield and frontal brainlobes with reflection of soft dark malevolent pursuit. Let me off and leave me younger, not to have even begun! I was bawling from tension of pure operation, impossible to keep back wheels in line as we slid the curves and screwed the straightways. Faster and more fast, let me lift off the roadway into leaves of the dark trees. The sky funneled down on either side to close me in with the face behind and concrete airstream ever onward.

My reflex solution: on with the radio and goodbye!

We're in that good soul bag brothers n sisters! Wipe yr tears dry yr eyes n groove me Grover with yr two left feet! O Mama can this really be the end! Drive me wild wild wild mah wild bayba, just like you did before!

And there was I, sweet Love Betrayed, struggling but why struggle, back home again on the sunset roads of boyhood America, truly truly with emotions all my own hacked off like ballpark hotdogs by the blade of empty rhythm. Old Doc Tyrtan perhaps heard Hindu music and drove along carpet-style easy as pie. But for me there pounded a mockery of dreams and yearnings as I re-endured through one generation after another the ultimate betrayal that broke our great big heart.

Dream! When ya feelin blue! Dream on little dreama thatsa thing t'do. Sky of blue life of ease friends aboard as we please, hey lifewubbea dream sweetheart!

Now there's nothin in the wurld but a boy n girl n luv luv luv. Truluv truluv gimme all y'got. Whenever yr near so dear to me babe Ah crahed ovuh yew babe yew R the 1.

Luv luv alone falling from the throne of Daddy n I don care I don care what peepul flink of me.

Ah think Um gunna B O-K.

Yea-hey the whole wurld in muh hands as Ah pass mister 5-16, revvin up his engines with the dragstrip queen, seventeen, dance all night, cumon bayba, do it right. Truck on hi, squeezin by, moonjune pie, dig my fast, lightnin' blast, rubber howl.

Have yuh talked have yuh talked to the man upstairs he wants to hear from yew? n the man behind with the blasted mind will he be comin too?

Help help help Ah'm feelin dow-ow-ow-own. Hold me! Squeeze me! Nevah let me go!

People think they tried to tell us a boy like me wantin yew we're too young no you'll never win no no no you'll never win. Hey sweet *never,* throbbin on n on! *You*'ll never win Daddy Ah make it now Ah pound Ah *go,* faster than yew know!

n underneath it all babe the truluv blues in the night in the rain in the parking lot all over again

yew n me mah achin heart threw with luv bye bye luv yew made me luv yew now yr gone. Ah crahed ovuh yew, yew sit rite down n crah the way yew made me crah babe whole day long. Tears fell like rain left all alone nobuda call me on the telephone an dear 1 where R U 2-nite?

Ah crahed for me, the lips she was kissin Ah was kissin then n Ah knew feelin blue that she'd never more be tru

with another gal with another guy with sum-one new in another town on a night like this

love me hold me 1 more kiss close mah eyes put mah head on mah shoulders n dream now nevah let me go

sun go down no one round on the outskirts of town

want yr luv *need* yr luv

but Ah'll get by don't ya worry don't ya crah don't ya step on mah blue suede shoes!

In the blackest night he is always near thump thump thump thump thump

It's mah party n Ah'll crah me a river, weep me a windfall, lonesome sparrow sings red robin bob-bobbin

gunna tell yr Mommy, tell yr Paw

'few don't do me right, do me wrong, cum n luv me booby all nite long

a poorboy like me, whole wuruld in his hands, Ah tried Ah tried real hard, the good book Ah did read bout yo lyin cheatin ways, n Ah say all mah prayers to the man upstairs, sang the blues swingin n surfin, for yew bayba, gimme all yew got, give it up give it up, time goes driftin by so slow-oh-ly n time all alone hey hey in the night will yew cum back sumday?

wurld go round up n down threw with luv

lonesome me

hol mah han

And so I fought off all by myself all efforts to sideline my ass, thinking, thinking, trying to sort my mind back from the Drug and the music and the highway of my junkpile past. And always as I drove the frantic inescapable exaltation I could not tell from panic, wherein my soul simply swelled with the sense of being swept on and on, whether to God on high or over the edge, whether chased or leading, whether in high pride's rejoicing or in disgrace, so that all men's eyes would be cast upon me, and none of it would be in vain. . . .

Unless it should stop!

I wanted to be left alone, without all this other! And yet to go on and on, never to stop!

We swung down a long stretch parallel to a raised train bed. And here came the train, a sleek metal pile-driver spewing black smoke against the blueblack sky, ripping alongside us one phonepole after another. I had my right foot flat on the floor in prayer with no thought of lifting it or a sense of choice even but only the logic of all my yearning which bloomed completely wiping out decision shoving me to keep on all the way to the final smash or out the other side.

Like going through a mirror I swung up and around to cross the tracks in one swift wrench of the wheel and went up off the ground with a flat black nowhere bump which hung me in the sky. Yet all the time I was driving, driving, I knew full well; and I had pierced the plane of the train's forward motion one instant before it plowed through behind me, cutting off forever the long long trail a-windin back to the land of mah dreams.

Way out there in the realm of game-existence, I featured Tyrtan as he saw the winds of karma blow a metal barrier between himself and my own lost soul. He had to sit, held motionless by a white wand, while an infinitude of material carriers sped by. Each one as it popped through the slot of his vision caught the light and released one bullet of glare, blasting the open pits of his pupils. He wouldn't bear it, went to his glove compartment for the dark glasses. Thus no one on the train could have identified him if false and malicious charges were later to be filed by a conspiracy of federal agents, border guards, railroad cops, college presidents, pathic puritans, U.S. armed forces, the mafia the masons the mothers and the medical establishment. He had forseen all this long before, had picked it up from freely-tuned-in vibrations —including those of radio-energy.

"HEADACHE? TENSION? CONFLICT? DESPAIR? *Vanish* in just five seconds or—"

He snapped it off, preferring his inner frequency. Across the surface of his shades the reflections of interminable boxcars went click-click-clicking away, as my ex-gurubabe sat immobile.

15

WHEN I REACHED the outskirts of town the clouds shook out a few last drops and zipped up tight. A freak spring morning was underway, with Dr. Tyrtan not in sight.

Over in one corner of the sky the sun was shining, sliding long dustbeams under jagged blotches of cloud. Below, the surface of the earth was covered with bustling people like a crust of bread in an anthill. In short elbow jerks the shopkeepers let down their awnings, plopping bucketsful of rainwater across the streaming sidewalks. Men trooped briskly off to work, students wandered late to classes, women out buying vegetables proudly shoved their babies.

On the radio the holy subprelate mumbled prayers for the new day, that it might be registered along with the old ones. The drone held me in surround, body tired but mind in electric alert, expecting mortal danger at any instant.

Red traffic light seeping. Tried to force it back with my field of vision but it slipped up and let off an ultra violet fart. They honked me. No doubt it would begin now. A cop took one step and I flinched to bottom of my feet, my body curling like ash of a burning leaf. I tromped the gas, swerved round a corner, around another, and sat trembling in my tiny-celled auto under grained trees dripping Chinese water-drops.

Around me sat a tribe of neat houses. Homes. White board homes with brown Tudor beams. Very very quiet and sealed off little places set back behind plots of lawn and hedge or modest picket fencing. Each quiet little house shut up tight—doors shut, no one peeping, windows locked, curtained—no dust inside. Little walks leading up to them and steps set just so. Open them up and out comes the horror.

Somewhere deep inside people opening their eyes. It was morning-time, fresh new morning, when each man must see the morning light on the wall of his room and dare to remind himself who he is. Then pop out of bed, open the door very quickly, trot down the proper little walk without forgetting. By noon the horror would have vanished and you might do a lot of eating. But had a worm flipped out when you opened your morning egg? All your imagination!

I decided to abandon the car. Someday the owner would claim it, and someday I would buy Benjy another bike. But while I could, I had to try the simple trick of walking along the street. That was why they'd wanted me to stay. That quiet Nina—she would know I wasn't ready. The morning people walked toward the center like mechanical dolls. I couldn't make it. But I hadn't been wrong to leave.

I came to the place where people were crowding to buy papers, pressing, shoving, breathing each other. They breathed on me. And I shrank. Nearby an opening where metal teeth sucked them under the ground. I had seen that every day without realizing. And as I stood there radio static crosshatched me, plating a metal lining in my throat where I could neither lick it out nor swallow it.

I did walk then, against the current, carefully not stepping on the cracks, through the square and out to the quieter streets on the other side.

The sun was probing for me. It shone magically through holes of a peculiar building where people went to sculpt and paint and solder. Without choosing I moved in among the curves of glass and sky and textured concrete.

I walked straight up the pebbled ramp tongue, thinking to get gobbled and therein assume location. The sky above was strewn with bloody rags and patches. Birds shrieked like lunatics. Did they too have mini-souls shut up in their precious head-bulbs? Poor round eyes peeping jerkily on either side, fixed never to center on any one whole thing!

Inside a glass door I went, scarcely touching, and up a flight of scalloped steps, my own slam fluttering after me in curved glass waves. Behind me stairs twisted down like an unraveling lolly-stick. A floor appeared at level with my nose.

I saw janitor-feet plus mop. That a man could be content! I meshed amid folding glass to spy on the custodial, slipping deftly between cantilevered metal planes of industrial reassemblage. The man's nose wore a drooping mustache with thousands of dusty hairs. On his feet were leather casings from the skins of animals. With each sweep he reassembled a whole new particle universe. He himself was a particle, rhythmically in motion, orbiting his mustache through life as he orbited his wide dustmop. Not beautiful, merely continuous.

I popped around a corner and filtered into a channel that broke off sideways and up, lit on the diagonal by thin-beamed windows emiting long stripes of light. Clouds veiled the sun and unveiled, causing the stripes to flicker across me like knives. I screamed a little, and saw my screams wind upwards and diffuse themselves through whatever openings.

I ran out on the roof, a seed patch of bleached

stones, some of which sailed to the ramp and bounced high, settling on a pentagonal grassplot far below. I was way too high, higher than I had ever meant to be. Yet still another floor curved above me, directly over my head. Up one space and *then* will I define myself? Later. For now I crawled to the center of my cozy rock garden and looked down through a bulging plastic skylight. Saw a fountain, goldfish swimming up marble stairs. Around the fountain curved polyethelene benches where no one sat. Life is a fountain, that I remembered. But then what?

I jumped and got a handhold on the bottom of the ramp above. People on the sidewalk were looking—some pointing, some running up. I heaved my leg with all my might. The precise leg pleasure was definite, mindless.

A class was in progress as I entered an upper chamber and threaded through the painted putty, the enameled slabs, the rods and tubes arranged on finest wires. "Let's get this straight, once and for all," the teacher was teaching. "Art is art and life is life—there is *no* connection." So "Bravo!" I shouted and clapped my hands as I drifted through. The sculptures were flowers waving in a non-meadow, the students bees lugging depolinated pollen. When all was ripe they would cut up their collections and store the parts in a barrel marked "barrel."

I toed up a ladder on the side of the building which ended in a crevice too small for sitting or standing while above me loomed the point of the roof, tapering to one fat pin. For fun I lined up my eyeball to leave it there. Pricked open, would infinite glittery mirror grains come tumbling out, the pieces of everything I'd ever seen? No. I stuck my foot in the crevice, and hoisted myself with the pin in one hand.

I could see a patch of river down the street, flowing in a yellow rush swollen with rain and melted snow. The motion jangled me like a fire-alarm. Flow downstream! I hated those words. It was all too obvious the Big Bomb would drop and break all matter down again to its basic molecular structure. Why not this very afternoon, while the sun was blazing with heat of unforeknown apocalypse? Sad but true! Face up to it, middle class soft ones! I had gotten myself high on the last night on earth, to become the only one who knew.

Could I shout it to the people down below? Tell it like it is, bayba! But my voice dissolved in the wind, auguring massive dissolution of soul and body. The notion of communication clearly an absurdity; my function simply to know, and to register. But what point to that, if my spirit were meant merely to return to the home base, to mingle and merge in weightless spaceless etc?

For sheer spite I could have jumped again. All that held me back was something in the texture. The spire swayed in the breeze, tingled, letting out a metal whine. Whine away! I would hold till it cracked! Then blast your blast, old Bomb! Billow! Mushroom! I would hang right there till it came for me. Damned if I'd let loose—yellow stream flow your heart out!

A long clench later I found myself descending the ladder, which led to an areaway bounded by three curving trunks of the upper building.

No standing upright in that cramped space. And now from all around me came munching the echoes of voices. Reflections of people ran by not knowing how to get where I was. No up down or sideways: balconies, railings, shadows piled and staggered one on another till they cut off all outlets. I managed however to scuttle forward. The concrete slid cool against my belly as I wiggled into a long damp tube. Perhaps I could spaghetti through the heating-cooling pipes and pierce the very heart of the building. Or I might enter the wiring and pulse back out through a dynamo churning in the basement. Or liquefy and flush through the plumbing, trickling by the timid searchers in the halls.

I emerged instead upon a scooped sloped gully which curved gently down through long blank planes to empty out on a ground-floor alley. I settled sweet as rainwater, and hung at last by beltbuckle only, pressing grateful lips to the filthy wet gravel of the drainage bed. Releasing myself I rolled easily to my feet, my belly righting in a nauseating flop. I hurdled a back fence, crossed the lawn of a museum, and appeared once more on an ordinary sidewalk.

A bad thing began: black waves rippling from people on the street. I dodged, blinked, twisted, but still they came: radar storm waves of hate and anger. I couldn't let it build—must clamp down on it, show it was only a Drug-effect. A piece of reason: they did not personally advance on me, the people. But whenever one passed a finger squirmed in my brain. I cringed inward, though they gave no sign of seeing. Trained not to show? When they stared, as people will, their eyes were abysmal.

I headed for the park down by the river, recalling my last touch of comfort in the green lawn slime of the Heavenly House backyard. I wanted something natural and stationary to lean my head against so I could safely switch off my mind.

But above and below me a net of wires was humming, with electrons chafing like flocks of angry wasps. Though I had blocked it all my life I now could actually see the power streaming inside wires from building to building, activating washers, heaters, garbage-gulpers, cookers, listening-boxes, switchboards, microphones, earplugs, hot-blankets, tooth-grinders, pants-pressers, stitchers, coolers, dryers, cleaners. And then the words, reports, instructions, denunciations, zooming above through the air I breathed and submarining the earth I walked upon! TV-tubes, transmitting what images they wished! And the mail shooting by in secret trucks, unloading words at a central station where they mixed, sorted and shot back out again without the slightest check! And the mailmen, the doctors, streetcleaners students repairmen—all carrying bags which they opened to dispense or re-collect! A blue gas glowed from the drugstore on the corner, where your friendly pharmacist ground and mixed and reassembled his hairy molecules for the resexing of all known organs! Over at Aunt Ma's Eatery they cleaved off slabs of animal in the back room, to treat and heat and serve to other animals! Locked to stools they reprocessed their particles—then let loose of them, dropping them down a maze of pipes under homes and streets headlong to the river, where they rambled out to sea or filtered back to land again. Or lo and behold a new organism might blossom inside one eater, only to be released in turn into the atmosphere, pumped full of liquids, boxed and medicated in the very facility that nursed used-up organisms till they were shipped for redistribution inside the earth.

The humming I heard, the mixing of messages and vitamins and particles, was the surface sound of a gigantic fabric interwoven not by accident but by specific design to enmesh and control me. This was my vision—just as powerful natural and obvious as any vision before. But which was true? Why all of them! I'd simply been blind till then—and why not, that was Tyrtan's function—to the fact that the ecstatic order of the universe was just a sugared mockup for the vicious earthly mesh which now held me fast.

And all the time I heard two voices fighting in my ear for control of me. The first said, you are under the influence of a drug. You have no way to measure. It will all seem different, later. That first voice was straining to drown out the second, but the second only laughed, and whispered in a cutting undertone: You know now what you knew all along but never faced up to. You took the Drug only because you were ready. The system, the energy of the system is everything. People keep from insanity only by shutting out that energy. But you, o noble piece of turd, you let it in, and you will never again live without it. From now on you cannot go in the street, or talk to another person, or even read or listen, without being yanked by the tug of empty mockery. You will sleep suspended between the electrodes of a humming magneto. Your mind will be a sealed box of madness and confusion. Because all is atoms and the play of light. The world will blow apart, and scatter like so many grains of sand. Because everything is truly blackness, the drunkard, the dog, the Void, the pit, nada, nothing. . . .

I came to rest at a barber pole, into which I stared absorbed, cut free at last from time and place and the people who passed me by. The Answer lay now in the red and white stripes that twined across one another in a ceaseless interweaving, while all the time retaining their constant, impeccable boundaries. Just so the interminable spiral winding ever upward, yet contained within its hermetic cylinder. The tube's pristine stasis was repeated among the rods and cones of my receptors, creating a caressing sameness on the picture tube of my brain surface. Once more my vision was just as logical, just as real. . . . It came with its own faint whirring music, in which I could detect the tinkling of concentric Ptolemaic spheres, tissue-thin, one sneeze and God's glory shatters. I understood that now. The picture was complete, but from the outside I was dimly aware of an infinitude of other ways. . . . Which bothered me, or rather, would bother me as soon as I moved, and thereby transformed my inertia into an assigned velocity exposing me to the deadly mesh of the networks. Better to stand, while I could, and contemplate my cylindrical Oneness superimposed on the turning axis of the self-enclosed spiral. Until the barber came out to inquire, innocent razor in hand, and startled me off the edge of the cylinder and out again into the murderous planes of day.

Having threaded my way through a series of right angles, I stood clinging to the rail fence along the sidewalk bordering the river park. The river rolled beneath me like a brown hillock in the full light, glistening with patches of sun. Avert myself, lean away from that glistening! Dogs romp too along the river bank like fanged beasts escaped from beneath the earth.

I would have run but for coincidence of Cathy down walking in the park with Huckleberry. As usual she slouched, wearing pants too so that even at this distance I could see the imperfect space where the tops of her thighs should have joined. Huck, having learned to walk that fall, was having at eighteen months his first uninhibited outdoor ramble of the winter. He rolled along like a sailor elbows out and rubber pants ballooning, while his mother strolled behind him, unconcerned, drooping a little, glancing now and then at the river or the sky.

I was swept by an unaccountable tenderness. Why account for it? I ran down to them, and she was pleased, I could tell, truly pleased to see me.

I hugged and squeezed her precious upturned stem. She was laughing but at the same time she could feel, I knew, it was too much. The desperation of my coming on! I knelt as Huckleberry toddled up. Beamingly the little manchild took the pretzel from his mouth and offered it to mine. I grabbed the soggy morsel in my hand instead and searched hard the boy's big murky eyes, brown with gold flecks and reflections of dancing trees. He withered of course from that stare, his downy eyebrows curling at the inner ends and wide eyes frowning. What kind of Alex was this? With a grunting sob he snatched back his pretzel and went on his way.

I had to tell Cathy everything. I needed help, but it was all so changed!

"What's the matter?" she said. "What is it?"

"A veil torn away!" I burst out in clacking laughter, ugly and impossible to hold back.

"No, not that," I said. But what to say? "Our whole lives," I said, "we can't go on. I mean everything has to change! Because of you, in a way. But I'll have to quit school, travel off somewhere maybe. To California or Algiers. If we should never meet again it will still turn out all right."

"You went to that place, didn't you? You're still very high."

She knew that! But of course she would know!

"Were you worried about me?" I asked.

She shook her dark head, glancing up at me in quick mild calculation.

"No," she said simply.

"Because you never thought I'd take the Drug!"

"I thought you probably would, sooner or later. But I was sure you wouldn't hurt yourself."

"Why not?"

"You usually don't." She squeezed my arm.

"You mean I don't keep going, really lay it on the line! That bugs me," I said, "—that you could think that, after all this time!"

"No, not that. But you do have a certain . . . oh . . . cherishing for yourself. It's not a bad thing entirely."

Not entirely? What were we talking about? I couldn't follow. . . .

"What about Benjy?" I heard myself ask.

"I couldn't go back," she told me. "The baby's had a virus. Nothing serious, but I had to stay with him. I phoned your place but no one answered. Poor Huck was really wretched that first night. Today's his first day out, and even now I wouldn't bring him if it weren't so warm. It's like spring, remember?"

She slipped her hands into mine.

"But he looks all right, doesn't he?" Huckleberry was waddling far ahead. "Benjy's probably all right, too," she said. "After all, it's been three days. And it is *so* lovely! Just smell! The air's all fresh and clean!"

Despite the banality she was right. These three days had rolled up my whole lifetime. Benjy could not possibly be the same as I left him.

Cathy listened most attentively as we walked along. I could see she was amused and concerned, yet not alarmed in the slightest.

"But do you really understand?" I demanded.

I faced her and made her stop. We had pulled up alongside Huckleberry, who had got a stick and plopped himself in the mud for some prodding and stirring.

"Yes," she said. "I understand what you're saying. But mostly I think you're terribly high. It really doesn't make sense you know."

"It doesn't!"

I was glad to hear it in a way; I made her say it again. "But why doesn't it?" I demanded.

"Oh, it sounds like what they all say."

As usual she felt no need to be precise. She tried to take my hand again, but I pulled it away sharply.

"That's just it!" I exclaimed. My voice was grating, and I believe she tried to shush me. People were mildly looking as they passed.

"They talk that way because they know," I insisted. "I knew myself but could never admit it, because of my would-be identity as an intellectual. It's an odd thing, but you're one of the main people who pushed me outside that."

Her head was drooping slightly; she was smiling her mild little smile.

"For instance those times we've been outdoors—and you won't let me speak, you stop me—because everything hangs together! And I had to stop and see that! Like the day you made me look at a single leaf. You were trying to open up a vision. Well I've got it now; I see that vision; I see a unity that folds in every goddam blade of grass!"

"Well everything *is* together," she said. "But that doesn't mean there's anything magic about it, anything beyond."

"The beyond is inside!"

And she gently laughed at me.

"You don't understand!"

"No I don't," she said. "But I don't assume. I've never had to. And when I look at a leaf, by the way, I just look at a leaf."

That made sense too. I had to laugh. I knew what she meant. And it bothered me. What was it I had to tell her? I was coming down.

Huckleberry had come upon a group of scruffy winter pigeons, strutting exactly like himself and bobbing their heads for a windfall of soggy breadcrumbs. When the pigeons saw the shieking arm-waving little man bear down on them they lifted cynical wings and sailed a few grudging yards in the air. Huck began systematically to pick up the crumbs and pop them into his red round mouth. He chewed absentmindedly as his mother got hold of his hand and steered him off without attempting to snatch his prize away.

I picked up a twig. "Here, Huck, see where the buds

will come out and then the leaves! It's the wheel of life!"

At that he burst out crying for real. I shrank, in fear he would disintegrate, scatter on the waves of his own shrill sound, melt with the pigeons in patches of slick dirty snow. Terrified, I clutched Cathy's free arm.

"I can't face it!" I told her. "I'm afraid to give up my pitiful ego. I'm afraid to let loose and not be me!"

"I wouldn't worry about that," she said.

"Just stay with me!" I pleaded. I made her promise not to leave, to let me tag along for days if I wanted.

We walked along in silence as I clung to her. Up above I had the impression of a definite spot, a stain in the air that contained the essence of all soul-matter. Once I died or was killed—and that would happen soon, I knew—my spirit would rise to that spot and hang forever in an ecstasy of nothingness. I would have no self, no memory, no intelligence, no anticipation: nothing but pure luminous consciousness. And the truth was I dreaded it. I couldn't tell anymore whether the knowledge had come from within or from Dr. Tyrtan and his holy book. I simply did not want to go to that spot. Yet I dared not stay away. If it existed, and they all knew about it, accepted it—then they were braver. They had gone all the way. They could live their lives right up against the Truth. They could make a fool of me and anything I said or did.

Over the river a rainbow was forming. But I couldn't watch; I had to stumble along head bowed and eyes fixed to my shoes. Ridiculous objects, shoes. The shape of them, so like the feet. . . .

Cathy had stopped to let Huck pat a dog, and I was aware again of all the faces. Almost right away I saw Bunny from Kansas City, boot up on a bench and talking to . . . Renée. She wouldn't look at me. But Bunny nodded in his pleasant way. Funny I'd never appreciated the kindness, the genuine tact, of his politeness. Renée sat primly like a little girl in white boots with her knees together and a very short skirt. Now I didn't know of any sexual thing with Bunny and Renée, but there must have been something. And something more. Because as I watched, the ruffled blandness of Bunny's strong clean features twisted into an animal pain. Bunny had a great tormented soul! Bunny, of all people, in his little mod cap! As much as I did, he knew! Of course he knew, and had always! And the others in the park—the boys sailing a plastic pieplate, the girl reading, the old man taking five minutes to swing one foot in front of the other—they all knew! The fixed expressions, the habits, manners, talk: all were masks to hide the essential consciousness.

Because it would have been too terrible if they suddenly broke down and communed on a level of total awareness. It would be the end of the day, the end of the city, the end of the river. Because then they wouldn't be able to follow through with the ridiculous things they were doing, like tracing words on a page, worrying about exams, feeling sick or happy, fixing hair buying clothes chewing gum or thinking all the millions of thoughts about whether anybody loved them or would they get laid or die of cancer or make big money raise their children crash in a planecrash. All wanting things! All fearing things! And all hiding behind horrible grotesque masks, like Bunny's cleancut nobility or Cathy's competent womanly concern! They were grotesque because they *knew,* and they had to hide it!

Yet it was lovely that they knew, it was certainly that. The girl Renée smiled at Bunny just then—her two front teeth were of different colors! Why had I never noticed that marvelous bit? Nestled my boat in her harbor but never knew, because I couldn't bear it. Couldn't bear the consciousness it betokened, exactly as unique as mine, stemming from that same knowledge I saw now passing between Bunny and the girl and blessing them, making holy the lips with which they spoke. Their actual words were trivial, but so what, they didn't matter.

Although to listen to them made me sick. (Pause.)

Oh there was no deny: I hated them, hated everyone along the walk, everyone in the town, everyone I had known in life and everyone I would ever know. Because they chose to hide and stay ugly! I could have killed them for it, happily, without a twinge. Because they would not See. Because they would not know what they knew. Because they had turned away from the Infinite Self, and chosen instead their petty twisted ugly existences.

I would kill them by order of Dr. Tyrtan. Dr. Tyrtan would be elected President, and then all who would not See would be put to death. I myself would do the killing, and when I finished I would kill Tyrtan last. Tyrtan had no right to become President, once he had Seen. He had no right to wear a mask himself. Power and killing were the ugliest masks of all. And all who wore them should be put to death.

Cathy was off chasing Huckleberry. She swooped down and made as if to pick him up, but he shook his stubborn head and rambled on. Cathy watched him go. He was already dirty beyond repair as he elected to join a pack of sniffing yelping dogs. He was going to be a dog himself, and trundled after them as fast as his stumpy legs could carry him.

I grabbed Cathy and turned her toward the river. I wanted her to see the people, see the writhing of their faces as they struggled to keep the vision down. And out on the river the rainbow was fully formed. That too!

"There! Do you see?"

She shook her head. I let her go and damned if she

wasn't smiling! The smile meant that she saw, but she had to hide it from herself.

"You do see!"

"I see a beautiful day," she said. "But that's not what you want, is it?"

How did she know what I wanted?

She tried to slip her arm around my waist, to make me forget.

"I'm sorry, Alex, but beauty for me is just a part-time thing. Otherwise how would we ever know it?"

"But that isn't it! That doesn't explain it all!"

"But I can't explain it all!" she said placidly.

"Yes you can! *I* can!"

Her smile turned puckish.

"Then explain what that rainbow's made of!"

I was stumped: utterly shocked.

"You know, I can't!

"Basically I know everything," I added; "it's just the fine details that bother me." And I went off into a laughing jag.

"You need a meteorologist," said Cathy.

"I need a cold bath."

For a while I almost felt good. The vibrations were dying down, people receding back into themselves. Song birds singing, here and there a tree branch truly popped a bud. The air was good smelling.

But it's a false front, I thought. Had I forgotten that the world would end that day? It certainly had picked a fine one to go out on.

"But how will I live without the Answer?" I cried out mockingly. Beneath the laughter I was really in pain. But I made a fool of myself and got Cathy laughing at me too. I had to hold onto a bench to keep from falling down with laughter. And all the time there was a little voice inside calling *help help*. I wanted not to be high anymore. Suppose I were really losing my mind? Then Benjy and Cathy and the others would understand what a struggle I'd had all along. They would come and visit me in the asylum. They would speak of me in awe. Perhaps I would even get shock—and go right through it.

But was that what I wanted? Was I the person who wanted that? Then I must stop this crying out. Even Tyrtan had seen that.

Yet all the time I was laughing. "How will I live? How will I live?" I chuckled inanely.

Couldn't stop it. Cathy sat beside me rubbing my neck as I held my face in my hands.

"Can't you see how awful it is?" I laughed.

"Oh I can," she tittered. "But it's funny. I can't help it, it really is!"

Remembering Huck, she twisted round to look over her shoulder.

"Alex look!"

Further away than I would have thought possible, five or six dogs were trotting in a circle. And in among them laughing and yelling for joy was the dirty-faced Huckleberry. He lunged for a sniffing whippet, fell flat on his face, carefully pushed himself up and launched onward with his blocky belly. The dogs seemed startled but basically accepting. They sniffed Huck democratically and danced away at his pawing as they danced from one another. Round and round they went in the oozy mud, yelping and snapping and dancing.

"Alex," Cathy said, *"he's not high!"*

I suppose Tyrtan would have disagreed. Huck's rosy dirty face was radiant with unpremeditated glee. And lucky for him he didn't even know it. We caught him presently, and despite his protests Cathy was soon absorbed in reconstruction.

All this time the birds were singing and the sun was

shining and people were going about their business. I didn't quite know what to make of it. I leaned on a tree and gritted my teeth, bracing for the next Revelation.

"But I don't want to be stunned," I told Cathy. "I just want things to leave me alone."

She smiled nicely; she was busy combing mud and pretzel from Huckleberry's hair.

"I'm afraid to go to my room. Don't want to be alone. Not ready yet for just plain nothing."

Again Cathy smiled and nodded. She didn't realize how completely desperate I was. There seemed no choice between blank aloneness or total exposure.

"I'm going to go now," I announced.

Huck was trying to go too, in the opposite direction, and she lunged to catch him by the back of his coat.

"You'd better get some sleep," said Cathy a little devilishly.

"You don't mind my going?"

"Of course not. You ought to go."

"I mean you're not worried?"

"No," she said. "But do be careful."

She managed to give me a quick kiss.

"Love me?" I asked.

"Yes, silly. Now do go home and lie down."

Huck broke free and toddled squealing for a great mucky puddle. Cathy had to chase him; "I'll call you tonight!" she shouted as she ran off in her funny girlish half-run.

I climbed the bank a little sore. Like always, I couldn't quite get through. I couldn't convey the danger. But I didn't quite believe that either. What was it then?

When I got up to the street I turned and looked for them down in the park. There she was, walking along casually, with her legs a trifle far apart. She turned and waved and got Huckleberry to wave his fat arm. As if we were out on a picnic, and I the young husband sent back for a jar of pickles!

Oh but it was sad though! Suddenly my body warmed, and I could have gushed out vapid tears. The two figures were so set off alone, the boy waving and his mother kneeling at his side. They were fixed in the beauty of the transformed park as in a tableau of a scene which had once existed and could never come again. I had the sense of an exquisite memory, drifting ever just beyond the reach of all my striving. I was terribly unhappy. For all my love of Cathy I felt our contact fading, softening out, as a rainbow softens in a blue sky.

It was clearer than ever that I must rip violently away from my environment. To open up, to move onward, to make use of all I had seen and learned, I would have to make a drastic change. Or else it would all be up with me. An old thought, but I couldn't help it. There was another old thought that was even worse: that all would stay the same, and I would have to go back after all and fight a thousand little battles.

—Which was why I flinched from Cathy's lively smile, why I shuddered at her casual wave goodbye, why I turned embittered from her refusal to be scared for me.

I had started across the street when from far up the line there came a brilliant flash of light! For one instant I thought the last great bangup had begun, and froze to the white line. But it was only the glare from the roof of a jolting bus, which on its destined path would stop for me, to take me round full circle. Bright cars whizzed by on either side, flapping my coat, spinning me. Breathless I leaped for the curb, clutching my stomach. One of the cars had been black, with Dr. Tyrtan at the wheel. Or was he in the jet fighter plane that drew a single line across the sky? I lay my chest and stomach against the metal bus stop pole, and hung to it bravely as I waited.

16

BEAUTIFUL BEAUTIFUL in my seat along the river like anyone else looking out upon the glamorous day. A breeze breezed up enveloping the bus and streaming through the window a whiff of snowflowers. Fleecy clouds rode through the air like dragons. People were acting smiley to each other, swooning straight away as they sunk into their seats. This was one of the good days when things worked out. Maybe it would last and last, time all subjective anyway.

It all comes out in the wash. Example of my brilliance. Now what could I see with my big brave awareness? Observe carefully. A place for everyone on the bus—and as new ones enter, old ones exit. Non-linear rearrangements, transcending the old Aristotelian pigeon holes! Across from me a pair of young lovers, not students coming on to prove but townies in dumpy parochial maroon who therefore loved truly. And a spacious fat woman in clean fat summer dress daring singlehandedly to spread herself beyond the subject-object barrier. An old man looking happily out a window—both old and happy. Which proved that if you hung on long enough you learned a way after all for old folk to fall asleep at night.

Boomeranged to the end of the line and back, and what you know, the fear had lifted, tired and foggy but no more piercing jangle in the pit of my stomach. The motion of the bus had steadied me. The ordinary coming and going. Why not, why not?

But there was the bridge, and on my brainscreen flashed a slide of Benjy shrinking. As if I would hit him!

So that was in me, yes, that too. Even more so than in most of the troupe at Heavenly House. Or why else put them down? For not having the power? Who really thought they did? Deepdown we knew they didn't matter, or else why dance in a ring with microphones and flashbulbs? No they were only more people on a bus, whether seated or standing, quiet or yelling, dozing dreamily or churning inside with ruptured fetishes.

What I'd been after didn't come in packages. There wasn't going to be a Hand, to hand it to me. I was part of something more than warm pure dull good news. Now at last I'd got the rebirth message—and godblessamerica, there was my own name on the return address! The need again—and it didn't convert me. The Messiah bit was for fools of all sorts always. And if they were content, if they were happy, if they were powerful, if others believed them: the more fools they!

I was going to be stuck again, I could see that. At my most high I'd thought myself identical with everything else. But what was it thinking that thought? A puny human organism wanting like all the others to think itself omniscient, ubiquitous, immortal. The organism had yearned for comfort, deathly comfort, and arranged its thoughts accordingly. But when I opened my eyes, the details were still there, apart from me.

We'd stopped for a red light alongside a bar, that is a saloon, a noxious middle-class dispensing station for a stuporous addictive depressant doncha know?

In fact it was a place where we'd gone often, to escape the quad—a long dark room with neon signs in front, a big wood bar and bottles and a mirror, fronted by a row of sodden working men with hats and heavy dark coats sagging on their stools and on each other, bleary-mouthing, fading hunks of overcoat decay. Behind them ran a row of wood-partitioned booths, ending in a TV stuck up near the ceiling. Further back was a big room with tables a pinball machine and a jukebox. It was our affectation to sit at the remotest back table, where I leaned absently in my chair while Seymour or Benjy or someone talked on and on. Looking in now through the daytime window I saw my favorite bartender measuring out a drink. I used to watch that man; for he was of another order. A slim man who rarely spoke, very erect and exact, distinguished grey hair from fifty years of serving. It seemed he loved to serve. He loved to make drinks quickly and exactly and to keep the bar neat and to control the men.

That bartender stood out for me now, and I was startled to think that here was a life spinning out on the very next track from mine, that had nothing to do with the issues and images! No part of change except for sinking deeper in his sameness. And I saw him again as I had seen him so many times quite late at night, after his relief had come. He would sit at a table just for him and look off into space, smoking one cigarette after another in his long elegant fingers. He would light a cigarette, drag on it and hold it just so; exhale the smoke out into the dark and sit staring through it. Whatever was he remembering? Perhaps a woman, perhaps one time when there'd been love, and home. Perhaps a son, like me, and just as worthless, just as frantic, shallow, gone. . . .

Because he's old, I used to think. *And because he's you.* The soul does not expand it only ages, like whiskey in a barrel. Then it's tapped, and runs into a thousand gullets. . . .

I wept for that bartender; I wanted to go and kiss him.

Like a suitcase I snapped my eyes shut with all my tears inside, and immediately a strange scene took place in the theatre of my eyelids. Dr. Tyrtan and myself wore white suits in the lobby of a cavernous plastic hotel, while all around us tumbled roaring American businessmen, popping barbiturates and shouting great big hello's and how are ya's. Suddenly an angel in the pillbox hat of a bellboy. "Call for Doc-tor Tyr-tan!" And he hands him a snow white curleytoy on a pillow of inflated gold vinyl. Tyrtan listens. He's digging it, blue bulging eyeballs rolling like pinballs. "Too much, Baybee!" He turns with hand held over mouthpiece: "It's God"—with a sidetoss of his head.

"Oh."

The salesmen converge and commandeer the phone. "If you can't hear Him," Tyrtan warns, "you're not with it Daddy! Head off the frontier man you're blocking the group-experience!"

"We hear and obey," the salesmen chorus. "All hail our ultimate executive!"

They hoist Tyrtan to their shoulders, march in and out among ballooning furniture, while a horde of secretaries night students and media researchers watch drooling through the plate-glass wall.

"Three cheers for Oneness! Twoness! Manifest Destiny! The New Environment! Love is Ramana! The Rising Masses! Awareness and Awakening for All!"

Tyrtan flaps loose a huge starspangled flag, which catches the breeze to reveal at its center a sacred bull with two tails two assholes and no head. "Are you hip!" the Doctor shrieks. "Holy Cow! Shazam!" And the bull turns doubly inside-out, reaming itself into the mighty bald eagle, which takes wing and flies through the roof, its brazen beak gaping to swallow up the atmosphere. And the swinging salesmen, ripping off their clothes, chant a song which begins with the beauty of the lillies and ends Christ Columbus in the Pause that Refreshes. Flowers! Rockets! Cocaine! Bananas! Napalm! They blow it to the heavens, each and every piece of us twitching to the big beat as we meatball through the air and come down burning.

"I thought it would be more than this," the bellboy casually complains, wiping a dab of shit from his eyebrow.

Somewhat forlornly I pick up the gold-rimmed telephone, and into the chamber of my ears there moves the freighted rushing silence of an empty railroad tunnel. From atop a flagpole, far above the conflagration, Tyrtan is grinning grinning grinning, with manic intensity straight at me, as if so clearly to say: "You and I, you and I . . . the only ones . . . who know . . . *the terror!*"

I lift up my thousand-pound eyelids; the fear comes and goes, firing dully. In embarrassed revulsion I fall to examining my sweater sleeve. If I close my eyes again I know I'd join the dance. But meanwhile the gleaming threads, the whirls, the knobs, the colors. . . . And all that. My only alternative.

Remembered when as a child I'd stare from my bed at the board floor thinking myself into an airplane at masterly height. You get fixed in another world—turn your head too soon and the old room isn't back yet, the past vanishes and all your landmarks. Let the decision come deliciously, break the spell of your own free-will—then scramble up and run for sheer glory of your living body, its motion, its realness.

Just so, I looked up, but found little to charm me. The metal window-stripping was corroded at the edges and fit improperly against the glass. The leather of my seat was snaked by minute cracks I feared to widen by the moving of my leg. The bus shook slightly as the wind increased. Tiny droplets blew by in a fine fury. On the outside panel small triangles of flaking paint stood out like plane flaps in the violet air. Clouds were collecting again and the surface of the river was flayed into broken spouts and brief small teacups. Panicked people more and more crowded into the hollow of the bus as it bore down like a missile on the college square.

Unable to face the wall of woven arms and trunks I abandoned my seat and went to stand near the lovers. My mood had badly slipped I knew, I was tired, fazed, as I peered closely for encouragement. But I saw this time no glory or movement or even possibility: only the acne on the sides of the young man's mouth, the bloated white underfat which puffed the skin of the young lady's face.

Above the fat woman now and dug with my eyes a wen encysted in the cavity of her neckbone, where it swelled sabaceously, plump with sebum. Like an excised frog the woman jerked her head, as if to twist loose from the leeching pain the spore dragged up from its roots. The happy old man had liver spots up the back of his neck and on his hands, where the skin clung toneless as cellophane. Anyhow he could smile—but a little too much: his hands flew to his lips to pull himself closed.

With the bus boring slowly the people stood rigidly blocking, rubbing by with coarse jackets, jabbing with knees and elbows, squeezing stomachs with hardboned rubber and faint twitch of erectile muscle. Were there Nazis who directed this? I reached in vain for a couple of office girls who stood blank-eyed and tight-hipped in prim needle-heels, lacy blouses, plastic lashes, carbon eyestripes and shellacked tophair. The mass closed in and caught me from behind in the breath of an elderly mouth-cancer victim discussing cinema with a lipstick-thickened urticaric whose jowls hung in blasted udders. Pus dripped from my beltbuckle where a sorry little colored boy had smeared his infected forehead.

The taste of disease and decay clogged in upon me and unstrung my eye-nerves. Everywhere I saw putty faces gape and slide, ransacked by purple splotches from inner lights of the bus. My vision of beauty and order was full refunded in an ugly gangrene that rotted my lips and flame-striped my lymphous membrane. No need no more of metaphysics to know why the human pet leaps and twists for to snap at a morsel of soul divine. Me, too: a famished flea-bit moon-baying soul-yelping whining scratching itching stinking leaping puppydog!

Having squeezed at last to the rear door I burst from the bus like a popping blackhead, and charged with all my front through icy pockets of twilight wind.

Darkness clattered down like a pot lid. By the time the boys descended to the dormitory dining room the night outside was a starless moonless black. It was going to snow again: I could feel the violence tensing in the air.

Later I sat motionless by the light of a single lamp. I knew who it was that entered: I had left the door unlatched.

"If only you knew," he said softly, "the love and care that went into your session!"

I didn't answer, didn't look—drawn tight as a fist around a black lump at the back of my brain.

He drew near, sat near me on the couch. He called my name and said soft things to me. I heard him talking but I did not turn my head.

"Alex," he said one time. "Perhaps I did not do all I could." It stopped for a while.

"I've learned something about myself, Alex."

Once more his hand on me! And then I did turn, and when he saw my face he rose abruptly.

I rose moving toward him. He backed off mechanically.

He didn't understand. What's the matter Alex? No reason we couldn't be friends. Talk things over. After all that had happened. . . . Anyone's entitled. If I would only—

But I wouldn't, you see. I wanted to grab him by the neck.

He backed up babbling, through the doorway to the unlit bedroom. Then turned to bolt and bumped into Benjy hanging in the dark. Benjy swung away as Tyrtan stumbled and swung back to hit him in the face, my old friend Benjy, three days dead, dangling by his own rep necktie.

Rather tasteless of Benjy to hang himself—most of those who knew him turned from the subject with a delicate shudder. But I didn't give a damn about taste just then—I got hold of that dandy man and threw him against a wall. I didn't want simply to kill him—I wanted to hurt him, physically, to smash him up against something just plain hard.

Soon he was screaming and shouting so you could hear him clear down in the courtyard. And naturally my fellow test-takers came running; they streamed through the halls and washed in waves against our door—running and running, running for the latest, anxious that nothing be missed. . . .

POSTSCRIPT

As it turned out I only bumped Tyrtan around a little. He was too scared, too soft, too much like me.

The cops came soon enough, but no one pressed charges. Tyrtan went back to his drug farm and a month later, on probation from school, I wandered down to Mexico and spent a year there, at first with Americans in Mexico City and later in a rural village. Then I came back to college to finish up. Eventually I became a doctor myself—a doctor of detail.

Acting on a word from me, Amber's family traced her to Heavenly House. But the girl was gone, and they could never prove she'd been there. She was found a few days later off Buffalo, in a boat on Lake Erie. She chatted politely when spoken to but never recognized anyone—sees other people as "externalizations." She's spent the rest of her life on a porch, not knowing even how taken care of she is.

Jacky Mayflower is a jollier story. At present he's the exciting young president of Intermedia, which holds transmogrification rights to all the popular new art groups.

Seymour today is the hippiest insurance salesman in Honolulu.

I never did marry Cathy. Wasn't ready for her,

couldn't come through—and while I was in Mexico she quickly found someone else, as she had to, I now see. So I gained the advantage of heartbreak with no fine print of marriage. I was free to continue, for a while, on the trail of the Precious Boy. Later, when the Precious Boy had died (of boredom and old age), I married someone else, and that wasn't easy either.

As for the Drug itself, the Drug is dead, as the kids say these days. They have gone on to something new, and scorn their druggie parents. They feel gypped and cheated; they want to live. They are going to raise up their own children differently. Here in God's Country, why not?

In the late sixties there was a terrific fire which burnt Heavenly House to the ground. Dr. Tyrtan was in Paris at the time addressing a conference on love and being. He relocated near Los Angeles, where he served as contact for thousands of new followers. In the seventies, when the Answer Drug began to fade, he lived for a while with fifteen acolytes in a walled estate up in Hollywood Hills, where they spent the day around the pool in simple Yoga postures, meditating, sniffing scents, and rubbing one another with aromatic flower petal oil. I understand Tyrtan is making plans to withdraw soon into an even more private existence.

As for the rest—there are so many of us, so many. Go out on the street and take a close look at us. Some say these fifteen years have wrought an incredible transformation. But you had better take a look at us one at a time.

As a species we have not slackened in the convolution of new gods and new troubles. I dreamt the other night we were sitting in a circle holding hands. In the middle there flickered a torch or electric spark of some kind. Behind us were ranks of others waiting to press closer or crowding around lights of their own. While we in the circle—we pawed each other, clutching knees and buttocks, mouth fumbling to speak, sincerely.

But the flame was a fake and even as we pawed and pressed and fumbled we were tortured in my dream by the thought that we might stand up and turn away, face one another, deal with our own selves—no matter how dear the cost or brief the time.